THE
FIRE
IN MY
BELLY

TOM SCHULTE

WESTBOW
PRESS®
A DIVISION OF THOMAS NELSON
& ZONDERVAN

WestBow Press books may be ordered through booksellers or by contacting:

WestBow Press
A Division of Thomas Nelson & Zondervan
1663 Liberty Drive
Bloomington, IN 47403
www.westbowpress.com
844-714-3454

ISBN: 979-8-3850-1334-0 (sc)
ISBN: 979-8-3850-1335-7 (e)

Library of Congress Control Number: 2023922721

Print information available on the last page.

WestBow Press rev. date: 11/30/2023

This book is dedicated to my ancestors who escaped the tyranny of feudal Europe to settle in the Midwest frontier. Their struggles in frontier life punctuated their faith with hard work, success, and failure. I am inspired by their efforts to adapt to change and live life well.

CONTENTS

I

The Old Country

PA SCHUMERHASS TROMPED DOWN THE ROUGH-WOOD BASEMENT STAIRS. He always enjoyed their fall feast, eating more than he should, listening to his family, and grateful his barns overflowed from the bountiful harvest. He confirmed the well wasn't frozen and checked the pantry and the other rooms, finding nothing amiss. *It's such a luxury to have places to store potatoes, corn, and canned goods. How did we live before? I never imagined I could have an inside well.* His thoughts began wandering through his life.

He tried shaking his head to clear thoughts about the old country. *We lived so close to starving or freezing to death that we believed it was the only life. Our new home is about as different as possible from that place. Sometimes I miss my friends. I never miss the Barron.*

He entered the furnace room while still shaking his bushy head. His oil lantern bounced shadows through the room as he hung it on an out-of-the-way hook before opening the firebox door. The glowing coals feebly added light to the tiny room.

"You need more wood and coal to get through the night, my friend."

From the coal bin, he selected several logs, barely fitting into the furnace, and placed them on the floor. He quickly split another into small pieces using his short-handled sledgehammer, wedges, and mule-like strength, careful not to hit the ceiling. Now, he filled the firebox, using the smaller pieces to provide heat until the family snuggled in bed and the larger ones, with a shovel full of coal, to warm the house until morning. In the morning, he would feed the furnace before anyone else rose to keep the house warm and cozy.

"Well, Mr. Furnace, here I am again, feeding you. We ate well, and now it's your turn. It's cold outside, so you, like us, need to feast." Pa tugged his oversized mustache, tilted his head, and listened to the rising and falling winter wind. The happy furnace showed its feelings by sending sparks up the chimney.

Next, Pa looked into the nearly full ash bin under the firebox. He used the coal shovel to fill two five-gallon metal pails with hot ash. He peered into the firebox again and observed ash overloading the grating. Two quick pulls on the grate lever shook ash into the ash bin with a satisfying fluff. He had filled the ash bin. He used his last two metal buckets, muttering silently; *Herman never cleans the ash bin.* The furnace felt so relieved after Pa cleaned the ash bin.

Pa's eyes watched the shadows dance on the thick, concrete basement walls. They had convinced him the massive walls would protect his potatoes from the summer heat and not let them freeze in winter. He reflected *it was worth the expense, probably keeping the house warmer, too. Putting this basement under the house was a big job. It is still hard to believe that all our neighbors helped since I wasn't known for being friendly back then. How fortunate I was that my tragedy didn't destroy me but instead….* Pa's thoughts returned to those dark days until he shook his head again.

Pa studied the red-hot ash buckets, not wanting to know if his friend, Orney, could predict that the thick concrete walls and ceiling would protect his house from a basement fire. *I will need to let these buckets cool before I carry them out. I'll do it in the morning. But, by then, I will have more to carry. Maybe I should get a couple more buckets.*

Now, Pa waited until the fresh fuel began burning. He fiddled with the ash-bin door to adjust air flow, more from a need to do something than to accomplish anything. *It's something that opening or closing the ash door changes the airflow and makes the fire burn hotter or colder. My old fireplace never worked like that.* His eyes meandered to the water temperature gauge. *No wonder Ma was mad at me.* The water wouldn't get warm until bedtime and the house afterward. *Maybe, if I'm lucky, the radiators will show a little heat soon, and she'll calm down a little. I should have added a little fuel two hours ago. Oh well, it's too late now.*

He sat on a small log turned endwise and leaned against a wall. He could see a few miniscule flames dance through the tiny furnace windows and, like always, wondered about the windows. He knew they weren't glass but never found out what it was. His thoughts turned to another time when a smaller and younger family celebrated a different harvest.

"Well, Mr. Furnace, I was the village storyteller in the old country. We gathered after finishing our work, and I told the old stories. Everyone always listened attentively. We went to different homes, stoked the fireplaces, and spent the evening laughing and joking. Sometimes, Gustav told of his travels to America years before. Still, usually, my neighbors wanted to hear, once again, about our brave ancestors. They were something, those people. Tough as they come, but with hearts of gold. I never did understand how the Barron came to rule us. It's a shame, Mr. Furnace, that people here don't want to hear my stories. I guess my language isn't good enough. But you always listen, don't you?"

One log gently whistled from evaporating sap and water, encouraging Pa.

The furnace tried its best to burn the fresh fuel but didn't have enough hot coals to ignite the kindling readily. Nonetheless, the furnace knew Pa would sit watching the fire. Maybe, if lucky, Pa would tell of their journey here. The furnace hadn't heard the story for a long time and wanted to listen to it again. Eventually, after the wood ignited, Pa would leave. But for now, the furnace was glad for the company. Not that it was lonely, for its radiators heard everything that happened in the house.

"Mr. Furnace, it started years ago. I remember it like it happened yesterday. Listen closely; I'm becoming an old man and may not remember it much longer. You're an important part of the story, Mr. Furnace, for you were born after we arrived. You're my ninth child and the only one still listening to me." Pa chuckled with mock offense. All his children listened to what Pa said, maybe more than what he didn't say. "That was a tough time for us. We disliked the Barron so much that we never even said his given name. I can't say he cared much for us either."

The furnace laughed, making a small puff of smoke rise into the chimney. It'll be a pleasant night, as both entered Pa's story like fleas watching it unfold.

The icy wind blew snow against the closed door. The ragged family joyfully huddled around a small, rough plank table, celebrating the harvest. Crops were safely stored or sold for high prices, meaning the family had money left. With his back to the crude door, Pa glanced at where he hid his money and silently mused. *We can pay our taxes to the Barron and get something nice, perhaps a bolt of cloth or a new rope. Maybe both, and I will still have money left for emergencies.*

The mud fireplace burned brightly, serving as heat and stove for the family. Pa liked watching it; he was proud of his building efforts.

Fueled by an ample meal, the children's laughter echoed through the tiny room. Pride swelled Pa's massive chest as he admired his wife and four children. *The boys are growing up. Luis is the quiet one. He is so dependable. Unlike our dreamer and troublemaker, Herman, Luis works hard and enjoys farm work. Edith and Mae will make fine wives someday. Ma does so well with what we have. She keeps some food on our table and clothes on our backs. How does she find cloth? I don't know what I would do without her. If only she weren't so thin. Our good harvest is due to everyone's hard work. Even my little girls worked, pulling weeds from the garden. Edith tried cutting wood without telling anyone. Most of her pieces were small splinters; several were longer than the fireplace.* Pa secretly cut them smaller but publicly bragged about her efforts.

Pa's mind filled with optimism as he contemplated the prosperous year. *Maybe this year, I can get everyone a shirt without holes.* He made their shoes from old rags, rope, worn leather, and bark. Mae was the family expert in finding dead animals with useable fur and hide. *Maybe I can save the hide from the calf and use it. If - a big if - the Barron doesn't claim it first.* His giant hand automatically clenched into a fist at the thought of the Barron taking his unborn calf.

"Pa, everything okay?" Ma was always observant.

"Just fine, there are no problems," was Pa's taciturn response. *At least not yet; there was no sense in burdening her with his concerns.*

A soldier burst through the wooden door without warning, loosening the cast iron hinges from the jam and the wooden latch. The broken door fell to the side as he erupted into the hut. He was in full winter uniform, complete with shoulder tassels, cloak, fancy hat, and a sword by his side. Snow dusted his magnificent mustache and his neatly trimmed hair. White gloves made his hands more threatening than effeminate. His heavy, leather boots shone brightly, and through the damaged doorway, the family saw several more similarly-dressed men standing at attention. Wind began drifting snow into the tiny house, now lacking a door, while the family shivered in the cold. The sudden breeze caused the fire to throw sparks into the chimney.

"What!" Pa rose to face the intruder. The others, startled, carefully watched Pa. His black, bushy eyebrows seemingly stood on end, his massive, clenched fists hanging at his side. His eyes narrowed until they were little more than slits. The furious serf's appearance should make anyone think twice about breaking down his door. Ma thought; *his uncombed hair and ragged beard make his eyes look like burning coals.* However, the soldier never acknowledged Pa's fiery stare.

"A message for Luis and Herman Schumerhass from our beloved Barron. Monday, at dawn, in one week, you're to present yourselves at his estate for induction into his army." Without waiting for a response or acknowledgment that the two boys were in the room, the soldier turned and marched, with his comrades, into the night.

Herman jumped up and, with Pa's help, fit the heavy door into the broken jam, blocking most of the wind and snow. Ma pulled from the corner several heavy, ragged comforters made from old rags tied together, giving one to each side of the table. At the same time, Pa reached for his tattered coat hanging on the peg by the door. The room cooled quickly despite the roaring fire. Ma tried using the last comforter to block wind from most of the holes around the damaged door, vainly attempting to keep the room warm. Everyone pulled their thin clothes tighter and put their coats on. Their necks felt the cold the worst. They tugged on their fur hats to cover their ears and necks and put on their mittens. The children put their hands into their tattered pockets and looked around, wondering what would happen next.

The fur used in their hats and mittens belonged to wolves that Pa had killed. He was tired of seeing them chase and kill chickens. The Barron strictly forbid harming wolves for some unknown reason, but Pa had enough and waited with a club broken from a tree limb. The pack attacked him, but his massive strength, supercharged by righteous wrath, soon beat back the snarling predators. He killed three instantly by hitting them on their heads. Several more limped away, whimpering after suffering a glancing blow. He immediately skinned the dead animals, saving the meat but throwing the inedible parts into the forest, which, he later found out, wild animals scattered the evidence. For several days, his family feasted on wolf stew, and Ma made hats and mittens from the hide. They used the rest for straps and ties. The hats and mittens were their only luxury. They wore them everywhere, even to bed. No one dared speak of Pa's exploits, not even to their closest friends, for fear of the Barron's reaction. But, like in all small hamlets, everyone knew and respected Pa for his heroics.

Pa threw several more pieces of firewood onto the fire, sending more sparks up the mud chimney. He had rebuilt the mud chimney several years ago and always talked about it. The wicker hut, plastered with dried mud on the inside and outside and a roof of straw, didn't keep much heat in or cold out. The weather quickly deteriorated the roof and outside walls, forcing Pa to spend hours repairing them. He often wished out loud that he knew how to keep the cold drafts out and heat inside. Even his beloved fireplace leaked most of the burning wood's heat into the chimney. However, the fire's meager warmth was often all that stood between his family freezing to death and living. Now, standing at the fire, his eyes followed the escaping sparks' journey into the chimney, their reflection in his eyes speaking to his deep emotions. His brow furrowed as he pulled at the right side of his giant handlebar mustache.

The others huddled on their wooden blocks, spaced around the rough plank table, while Ma reached for her tattered coat. She always put herself last, no matter what. Usually, her family never noticed since that was just how it was. Ma was a rather tall woman, emotionally and physically strong. She was still young, but the family's extreme poverty had already chiseled her once pretty face into more thorn than rose. She always pulled her hair back to hide how unkempt it was, hoping she might own a comb someday. She did her best, making everyone's clothes from whatever they could find, much of it scavenged from the Barron's garbage and cooking meals that rarely satisfied their ever-present hunger. Ma always paused to watch the baron's daughters and female servants in their tasseled carriages, with bells on the harnesses, when they went somewhere, thinking about their fancy clothes and plump bodies. Sometimes, she believed she could smell their perfume. She always shook her head after they were out of sight, quietly muttering, "They look nice, but look who they live with."

"We've enough wood for the night. We'll bring more inside in the morning." Pa spat the words more than saying them.

"Pa, is there anything we can do? They're so young! They don't even have beards!" Ma's voice quivered, her hands tormenting her coat's frayed edges.

"He wants more soldiers for his wars. I heard many died in his last campaign. He's calling younger and younger men, even mere children. These useless wars will go on until no one's left." Pa's words came like rapid-fire musket shots from a firing squad.

Mae huddled next to Edith. The two young girls shivered under their blanket, only understanding that something horrible was happening.

Herman laughed. "Will I get to wear a uniform?"

"Yes, with bayonet holes from the previous occupant!" Pa was even more upset than his angry response showed. He continually clenched and unclenched his giant fists, his massive muscles twitching in his tattered winter clothes and veins throbbing in his muscular neck, prominently displaying his anger. He was huge by birth and made bigger by heavy farm work. Ma always said he could out-work the mule and was more stubborn.

Luis stared stoically into the fireplace, never one to show what he thought. Being a serf for the Barron had already transformed his youthful zeal into despairing resignation. *This draft was coming. I'm surprised it took this long.* But he kept his thoughts private. Keeping one's thoughts private was the only safe thing in the Barron's fiefdom. Like all the serfs, the land owned them. They didn't realize there was anything else, knowing only their ties to the land and, by extension, to the Barron.

"What'll we do? They're so young! What can we do?" Ma repeated worriedly.

"The Barron doesn't want men like me because he needs us working his fields. The way it's going, he'll induct everyone, including you women. The land will only have peace when everyone's dead!" Each word barely made it past Pa's clenched teeth.

"I need to talk to Gustav." A thought kindled in Pa's mind; it needed more fuel before bursting into flame. "Get them to bed. I'll be back when I get back. Don't worry." He looked at his fireplace's bright sparks before abruptly turning toward the door. Ma noticed his resolute stride.

Gustav was the village elder, considered the wisest and most trustworthy of the peasants. He lived in a small cluster of shacks close to the Barron's castle, while Pa's hut was the furthest. The good news was the greater distance meant the Barron made fewer demands on Pa. The bad news was they lived at the forest edge where wolves frequently attacked their farm animals.

"Pa, you're not going to do something foolish, are you?"

"Ma, the only foolish thing is to sit here and wait!" Pa briefly paused, his hand on the door's remains. And, since his coat was already on, it was easy for Pa to force the door open before disappearing into the wind and snow. Herman and Luis jumped to put the door and comforter back into place.

The fireplace heat slowly melted the snow, turning the dirt floor into muddy, slippery sludge. No one noticed, even the next day after the floor froze, that their footprints had fossilized and would remain until the spring thaw.

"All right, children. We're going to read our Bible." Their prized Bible was their only possession other than the rags they wore and a few makeshift farm tools.

The honor always fell on Herman. The Barron only permitted the second son to have an education. Until the wars decimated his male serf population, he believed the oldest should work the land, the next son would go into the church, and the rest enter his army. Daughters were only good for marrying and having more children. The Barron decided everything, or at least thought he did. He directed his farmers on which crops to plant, how much wood they needed to cut for the winter, and when tools required sharpening. One day each week, every serf over five years old was required to work in the Barron's fields. They cut wood for his castle, repaired equipment and buildings, or cleaned stalls in inclement weather. The Barron also selected several women to work one day each week preparing food or cleaning. Army guards made sure they didn't eat or take any of the food and severely punished any serf they thought was not working enough. Sometimes, they punished them simply for sport.

The Barron demanded to see the infant before a child's formal presentation in the little chapel, bestowing its name and who it would marry. The Barron didn't know that his serfs also planted gardens, allowing them to survive the harsh winters. He never had enough interest in them to bother looking at their hovels, which, fortunately, meant he didn't see their gardens, and none of his officers concerned themselves enough to tell him. What the Barron didn't know about, he couldn't take.

The Barron was the oldest son of the previous Barron. Rumor was that he killed his parents and brothers. What the serfs did know was that the soldiers attacked each other soon after he came to power. This civil war didn't improve or worsen things for the commoners, so they ignored it. The Barron forced all his serfs to parade before him after firmly establishing himself. "These peasants stink," was all he said as he held his scarf over his nose.

The Barron changed over the next several years. He became obese, needing help to dress in his frilly clothes. He periodically drove his fancy carriage around to survey his little feudal empire boundaries, which the serfs believed was more to show off his power than to observe the people's condition. Serfs saw him going somewhere and then returning after a few days. Occasionally, other nobles in their carriages came to see the Barron. It was after one of his visits to a neighboring noble that the wars started.

None of the serfs understood the wars, only knowing their children had disappeared. They might have returned if the Barron properly trained his men, but he didn't think it was worth the effort. Besides, deep inside, he feared that if his soldiers knew how to wage war effectively, they might rebel and overthrow him. His officers, always well-fed and clothed, were never in the thick of the battle, only ensuring the ordinary soldiers faced the enemy. The Barron gave widow's houses and field allotments to new families, stipulating that the widow came with it. Everyone did their best, but there was never enough food left after the Barron took what he wanted for himself and his soldiers. Now, there weren't enough young families, making life much harder for the widows. The rest of the village cared for the widows as best they could; however, the widows usually died young.

The feudal estate was self-contained. A blacksmith worked and repaired the serf's few metal farm tools and the soldiers' many weapons. The Barron encouraged a peddler weekly to buy surplus farm products and sell cloth and other supplies. Serfs could sell any excess crops to the peddler, who usually was stationed outside the castle walls. The peddler's many wagons hauled purchased grain to nearby cities in other feudal estates. Naturally, the Barron extracted a tax on this trade. The peddler often "accidentally" dropped something, like cloth, as he passed a hut, only to be met by a child near the forest with a few coins. Every villager knew who had clandestinely bought the product and ensured the untaxed transaction made it to the owner.

The Barron's territory included four main villages. Pa Schumerhass's town was closest to the Barron's fortress and barely outside the undeveloped forest. Being close to the forest also made gathering firewood easier for the family. The other villages were on the sides of the castle, and the Barron's enemies often raided them.

Herman opened the Bible to where they had been reading, in the book of Acts. Usually, Pa found something to do outside when they opened the Bible. Ma put her hand on Herman's torn sleeve; "Wait. Please read Psalm 91[1] for me, please."

Herman started reading.

> "He who dwells in the secret place of the Most High
> Shall abide under the shadow of the Almighty.
> I will say of the Lord, "He is my refuge and my fortress;
> My God, in Him I will trust."
> Surely He shall deliver you from the snare of the fowler
> And from the perilous pestilence."

Something about that passage caused Ma's brow to relax and straighten her back slightly.

Herman finished the Psalm.

"He shall call upon Me, and I will answer him;
I will be with him in trouble;
I will deliver him and honor him.
With long life I will satisfy him,
And show him My salvation."

Ma kept her hand on his sleeve. "Reread the last part."

Herman repeated, "He shall call…"

Twice more, Ma made him reread the passage. It seemed the fire brightened with each reading.

Ma paused, then began. "Let's hold hands this time and pray. We call upon the Lord and ask You to answer us. We don't know or understand the answer, but as your word tells us, show us Your salvation!"

A small bed filled the wall opposite the door. The four children slept in a storage loft above the bed, the boys on one side and the girls on the other, separated by their meager supplies. One of their nighttime jobs was protecting their food from mice and rats. Ma and Pa slept in a narrow plank below. Their mattress was torn burlap bags stuffed with chicken feathers, straw, and lice. Numerous insects made the straw their home and feasted nightly on their hosts. The family learned to instinctively brush away the occasional rat or mouse running over them or their supplies, usually without waking up.

"Hurry now, up to bed you go. Snuggle under your blankets and hold each other tight to keep warm. Don't forget your rocks."

Each child rolled their rock from the fireplace, wrapped them in rags to keep from burning themselves, and laid them at the far end or foot of the bed. They each placed their makeshift shoes near the fire, hoping they'd dry and be warm in the morning, and carefully walked barefoot on the muddy floor. Luis helped his sisters up before jumping up. Luis started pulling himself into the loft when Herman, laughing, pushed him back. They kept their clothes on, especially their fur hats and mittens, to help ward off the night's cold.

"Ma, who will cut wood if Herman and Luis go to war?" Mae suddenly understood her brothers had to go away, maybe forever.

"Don't worry. The Lord has promised us salvation. That means He'll take care of us. I don't know how, but He will. I only hope your stubborn father…" Ma's voice trailed off before she shook herself and continued. "Just don't worry. Go to sleep."

"Ma, tell Herman to give my rock back. I need it to keep my feet warm."

"Herman, stop pestering Mae. *Honestly.*"

Ma sat on her stump, holding her head in her hands. Repeatedly, she quietly mumbled lest she wake her children, "Lord, Lord, Lord…" The fire consumed its fuel until it was only a pile of glowing coals, allowing frigid temperatures to creep into their tiny sanctuary. She threw her last small log on the fire, which now, sadly, provided more light than heat. Soon, Ma could again see her breath as the puny flames made shadows dance on the rough mud walls. She heard her children sleeping but knew she couldn't.

When dawn finally came. Ma rose from her sleepless vigil and gathered the last of their wood from the woodpile outside to throw on the fireplace coals, causing the flames to leap to life. She pushed the heavy cooking pot on the iron hook over the blaze. While the fire heated the kettle, she retrieved a bucket of water from the shallow well and propped the door back into place.

At least I don't have to thaw ice by dumping boiling water down the well. The wind has died down, and I think it might be a little warmer. Somehow, gratitude felt strangely appropriate to Ma.

Back inside, she mixed water with flour from a sack stored on the dirt floor, the gooey paste sizzling when she put it into the hot iron pot. Periodically, she checked the concoction absorbing last night's left-over grease.

This meal would be better if we had yeast or maybe preserves, anything. I wish I could give my boys more on their last few days home. Well, self-pity won't do. I don't want them to remember me like that. Nope.

The smell of burnt grease and flour woke the children, and they tumbled from the loft, quickly donning warm, dry shoes over their callused feet.

"Where's Pa?" Edith was the first to notice.

"He had an emergency. But we know what to do to start our day."

Herman and Luis headed to the stable. Moments later, Luis rushed back into the shack.

"The mule's gone! I just went out to feed her, and she's gone! The gate's firmly shut, and the fence is okay! I don't see any wolf tracks in the snow. What happened to her?"

"Calm down. Don't worry. I'm sure Pa has her. Breakfast is ready." Ma was unusually cheery.

Each child climbed on their wood block. Ma broke biscuit pieces for each one, placing them on their wooden plates. Their dishes were still on the table, like always, but, as customarily, they sopped up what little grease remained using their fingers. Ma saved gruel and a biscuit for her husband.

Once they finished, the children headed outside. Luis grabbed the ax while Herman picked up the cross-cut saw before marching to a waiting tree in the forest. The two boys cut branches off a tree and chopped it into short lengths before using the ax to split the larger logs. The two girls carried the wood back to the house, stacking some by the fireplace to dry. The fire would have been better if the wood had more time to dry, but they did what they always did with what they had.

"This would be easier if we had our mule." Mae never liked chores. But they all understood the danger of freezing to death without firewood.

Noon came, and they went inside. Ma had prepared a stew, using the last left-over meat and some vegetables saved from their feast. The children gobbled their food, their hunger magnified by working hard. Like always, there wasn't enough.

The older two tried not to worry the younger girls by hiding their concern over Pa's absence. Ma was distant, lost in thought, not noticing Herman jabbing Luis or kicking Mae's block.

The afternoon was the same, except the two boys rehung their rickety door. Ma busied herself, making more biscuits and grinding flour between two rocks.

"Think we can make this work, or must we reinforce the wood? That soldier kicked it into splinters. What do you think, Luis?"

Using the cross-cut saw, they made a rough-cut replacement. Then, with their knives, they shaped it. It wasn't a perfect job, but it must do for now. They finished by pounding loose latch nails into position before returning to the shed. While the boys were busy with the door, the girls shelled corn and filled several bags. The four worked together, cracking corn for the cow using the round rocks and helping Ma grind more for themselves.

The sheep's water wasn't frozen, but the chickens had stepped into and dirtied their water. Mae loved the chickens and usually cried when they butchered one. She carefully cleaned the trough while the chickens scurried around her. Occasionally, she stooped to pet one, carefully cooing and making clucking noises.

"Mae, stop playing with the chickens! We have work to do!" Edith never stopped being the annoying big sister. Little Mae made a face and clucked twice before drawing several buckets of water from the well.

It was almost dark when they finished and headed back to their hovel. On their way, they each picked up an armload of wood. Edith entered first.

"Pa! You're back! I was so worried!"

Pa's eyes narrowed, and his brow furrowed into even more bottomless-like chasms, if possible. "Luis, kill us another chicken for supper. Ma, parch as much cornmeal as you can." Luis knew whatever Pa was thinking was serious since they didn't have chickens to spare.

They ate in silence. Pa quietly pulled his shoes off and laid down. "Everyone, get some sleep while you can."

The overcast sky was heavy with clouds. Dropping outside temperatures pulled the last remaining heat from their little house when Pa woke his family with an urgency they had never heard before. "Up! Now! Everyone put on all your clothes, bring your blankets. Herman, grab the cornmeal bag. Luis, help me with the mule and sled. Edith, help Ma gather the things we need. Mae, make sure our fire is warm and toasty."

And then Pa and Luis were out the door.

Mae turned to her mother, "Ma, what's going on?"

"Hush. Don't worry, but do hurry. Bring the blankets. Edith, bring our Bible!"

A few minutes later, Pa returned. "Everyone, let's go quickly. And absolutely no talking! Only take what we need to keep warm and eat. Bring your knives, and, oh yes, Luis, bring our ax. Go! Now!"

Pa paused, felt every bump on the mud chimney with his calloused hand, and muttered, "It was hard building you, but now, well, maybe someone else can enjoy your heat." He picked up his money bag. *It is a good thing we had such a good year. Our "beloved Barron" can do without this year's taxes. We should have enough to make it.* He walked outside, entered the makeshift stable, and stroked his cow's neck. "I'm going to miss you, old girl."

He thought about bringing the cow but decided against it. The Barron might believe they would return if he saw the cow. Besides, it wasn't giving milk, and Pa didn't think he could butcher it on the road. The chickens made too much noise, and nothing else was of any value. For a moment, Pa looked askance at the sled. *I hope we have enough snow and ice for the sled. We don't have a choice; my two-wheeled cart won't hold enough. I guess if we must abandon it, we abandon it. It won't matter if we leave it here or on the road somewhere.* He returned to the sled.

Pa paused and looked around, drinking in the little mud wicker house, with smoke rising from his chimney, then the rustic village, peacefully asleep in the moonlight and swirling snow. In the distance, the sky was clear, although it was overcast above the houses. The full moon was rising and would soon be above the snow–laden clouds. Moonlight reflected from the bottom of the clouds, casting eerie, frightening shadows in the sky. On a far hill, the Barron's fortress loomed ominously. The bright moon, rising directly behind the castle, cast a dark shadow over the village.

In contrast, fields around the village looked fresh and clean under the new snow blanket. Somewhere, a donkey brayed. Pa blamed his shivering on the bitter cold.

Wordlessly, Pa turned and gently slapped the mule with the harness, pointing it toward the road, and they started West. The road, a frozen mud river full of ruts, snaked toward the Barron's castle to the East and meandered past the forest toward a seaport to the West. A prince, more given to wine than administration, ruled this walled fortress. Fortunately, his bureaucrats were capable, and the sea trading was so

15

lucrative that the city lurched on autopilot. The fly in the ointment was rising corruption allowed contraband trade. Eventually, the Barron would attack and conquer this nearby rich jewel, but until then, it stayed blissfully independent.

The women huddled in the back of the sled, the two boys in the center, while Pa sat on the buckseat. He had filled the sled with hay, loose-ear corn, sacks of grain, and flour. The mule struggled mightily to pull the sled, often lurching and slipping yet somehow managing to keep going. At times, Pa and Luis helped push it through difficult places. The family arranged blankets and snuggled into the hay, using each other's body heat to keep warm. Each tired child tried sleeping but woke at every bump and lurch in the frozen road. The rising wind swirled snow around them and muffled the mule's soft grunting noises while the falling snow covered the tiny family.

Every hour or so, they paused to rest the mule. It ate a little snow and nuzzled Mae and Edith. *That mule mindlessly trusts us, just like we must trust God,* mused Ma.

The rising sun saw the little family plodding along the forest edge when Pa turned off the path and behind some brush before pulling the mule to stop. "Everyone out. We'll stop here to rest. Get yourselves a little to eat. We live far enough from the Barron that he won't immediately know we're gone. The snow covers our tracks, but his dogs can still find us. We're much too close to make a fire, so do your best to stay close to each other for warmth. Hope no one sees us."

"Pa, what're we doing? I have to report to the army soon." Herman knew he was breaking the Barron's orders and understood the consequences.

"No one's going into the army. We're leaving." Pa was in no mood for questions.

"But Pa, the Barron..."

"Quiet! Rest! You'll need it. Keep the ax handy. I'm depending on you and Luis to protect the others."

Everyone huddled together in the sled except Pa. After the mule had rested a little, Pa led it deeper into the forest. A small running stream provided water, and a nearby patch of tall grass had seeds attached. Pa tied the mule's harness to a branch, threw a coarse blanket over it, patted its neck, and ensured it could reach water and food before standing back.

I hope I'm doing the right thing. We'll all die if the Barron captures us. I had to do something. I just had to. Gustav told me how, who to talk to, and how much to bribe each. He said others had done it, and I could as well. All my brothers died for the Barron; he doesn't care how many souls he takes! What did that scoundrel do two years ago when our crops failed? Did he reduce our taxes? What quarrel do we have with those people he fights? He captures a few, makes them quarry stone, works them to death, then they're buried, and their families don't know anything about it. I wonder if the stories of his dungeon are true. If I must, I'll fight with rocks! I want to die here, in the open and sunshine, instead of in the darkness, listening to his cackle.

His musing, silent to all but himself, continued as he lay against a tree with a heavy branch he could use as a club. Exhaustion finally quieted his mind, allowing Pa to fall asleep, albeit not without horrible nightmares. Fortunately, wolves didn't attack the family as they slept.

The rising, bright sun warmed the weary family but turned the road into a slushy quagmire. The warmth made their sleep easier.

Pa woke the rest of his family just before sunset. They ate, drank water from the stream, and restarted. The slush made it more difficult for the mule to pull the sled, forcing everyone to walk, their bark and rag shoes breaking through the ice layer and forming a muddy, slippery slush. Ma began carrying little Mae, who promptly fell asleep in her arms. Shortly afterward, Pa held Edith, who, while not falling asleep, struggled to keep her eyes open in Pa's arms. They wrapped comforters around themselves and huddled close for protection from the wind. The two boys led the mule, who became increasingly stubborn.

Pa knew they must walk to conserve the mule's strength. Soon, drifting snow covered their tracks almost as they made them, and Pa judged they were far enough from their hovel that the dogs might not find them. The snow made pulling the sled easier for the mule, although the poor beast had almost had enough. Pa broke ice from the mule's legs every hour and rubbed them down. He adjusted the remaining comforter on the mule to keep it a little warmer and healthier.

"We're far enough not to have to go so fast now. We'll soon be beyond the Barron's reach." Pa felt encouragement and excitement with every step. "Our hands hold our destiny, and we don't need that arrogant despot any longer," he said to Ma, who could only nod through her exhaustion.

Each day was the same as the previous day, now traveling by day and sleeping at night, burrowed in their little sled's fodder. The sun's warmth lifted their spirits as they trudged forward, but the rugged travel blurred time. Some days, they made only a little progress due to the cold and drifting snow, while on other days, they felt they had wings. The temperature occasionally rose above freezing but usually stayed below, keeping the road icy. They wordlessly met rare travelers, becoming another group of poor trekkers rather than fugitives or refugees. The road became steeper and rougher as they climbed higher into the mountain range. At last, they saw their goal after the road began dropping. The family would have been excited if they were not so exhausted.

Pa peeled tree bark several times with his ax and knife to repair their makeshift shoes. Pa used his flint and steel to start a small fire to warm their shivering bodies when he could. He carefully checked everyone's toes, hoping none were frozen; fortunately, their callouses protected them from freezing water.

"It's good we're almost there," Pa muttered to Ma, "We're almost out of fodder for the mule and corn for ourselves."

Now, they tried blending in with other travelers, hoping to look like they had done this before. Yet, no one said much, knowing the family looked more like renegades than the destitute fugitives they were. Everyone worried about the next step except Ma. She somehow knew the Psalm's Author guided their journey and protected them.

No one robbed us, nor did the wolves get us! We made it just in time, as we ate the last of our food. Pa thought as they approached the city gates. Merchants lined the road, all noisily trying to sell their wares to travelers and city dwellers. Now, it all happened quickly; Pa traded the mule, sled, and ax for several bags of supplies and a little money, talked to the guard at the gate, shook hands, and "accidentally" dropped two coins as he turned to leave. The guard carefully stood with his boot covering the money in the snow, watching the wretched family enter the city.

Pa confidently strode through the city as if he knew what he was doing, and soon, the port appeared. Pa spoke a few words with different workers before disappearing, only to reappear and motion his family to follow. Events accelerated as they boarded the first ship they had ever seen. Someone directed them to cower in a corner below decks, behind boxes, crates, and barrels of cargo, which gave only minimal protection from the ocean's fury.

Later, the family might tell of their stormy journey across the Icy Atlantic Ocean. With typical language difficulties, they registered with an immigration official in New York, who directed them to settle on the frontier. They made their way North until they reached the Erie Canal, entered Cleveland, and finally booked passage West on a giant sled. The family marveled at the ten massive draft horses pulling the lake sled and worried about breaking through the ice. Besides the six travelers, the sled carried gunpowder, muskets, steel traps, and other supplies destined for the frontier. It would return with furs for the East Coast, expensive but profitable trips both ways. The sled couldn't make many more trips before the ice broke up; already, there were patches of ice melt. Herman studied the sled runners' tracks as they sliced through surface slush.

At night, the driver pulled next to the shore. While he tended the horses, the travelers rationed their meager supplies. None of the family said much, yet, in their thoughts, everyone but Ma wondered whether their hardships were worth it. They huddled in the sled under the tattered remains of their comforters, using what little cover they found for protection from the icy wind blowing over the lake. Ice froze into their hair and clothes, giving them an otherworldly appearance. Pa looked especially frightening, with his beard full of ice. The fugitives could see their breath before the wind quickly blew it away. Everyone tried covering their faces for protection from the cold, and Mae didn't dare tell her mother about her scratchy throat. Instead, she kept her mouth shut and burrowed even deeper into her comforter, curling into a fetal position and trying not to cry.

They finally reached their destination, a port in the largely uninhabited area of the Northwest Territory. Their lake journey was during the last winter storm. Now, spring struggled to burst forth while melting snow turned the crude roads into a soupy mire. Pa disappeared, only to reappear with renewed confidence. "This way," he proudly proclaimed.

The travel-weary family stumbled down a corduroy road constructed of tree logs laid in the swampy mud. The federal government had built the road, hoping to turn the inhospitable wilderness into tax-paying settlements. Pa single-mindedly forced his family onward, determined to avoid capture and be forced to return to the Old Country. At night, they struggled to find a dry roadside place to sleep. Most of the time, they were unsuccessful, sleeping in muddy slush. Mae and Edith tried to keep walking, but they tired quickly, forcing their parents to carry them.

At night, Pa set up a crude trap that occasionally caught a small rabbit. They could see the trees starting to bud leaves and hear an occasional songbird. The signs of spring encouraged Pa, but Ma only wanted to stop. She had to keep going until they got to a settlement. Herman amused himself by throwing mud at Luis, who occasionally punched him. The two girls were too tired to think.

Mae's throat felt better. She knew she had had a fever, which now was gone. It took several years before Mae found the courage to tell her mother of her illness. She did not want to be the reason they did not reach wherever they were going.

Finally, after traveling three arduous weeks on the corduroy road, Ma quietly approached Pa. "We can't keep going. We must stop. We're out of food and exhausted. Look how thin we are! Can't we find someone to work for? Please, before we all die!"

Pa paused. "The man at the port said there was a small village ahead. Please don't give up; we can make it. It's almost spring, and I should be able to find work. Gustav said they pay people with real money in this country."

The next day, Pa started gesturing like a little kid begging for candy, "Do you smell that? There are cattle close by. I can hear some. It sounds like they need breakfast, or maybe they are playing in the sun. That herd has to be huge to make such a strong manure smell. This forest is so dense, and the branches overhang the road that the sunlight can't reach the road. They are incredibly thick in this stretch.

Here, let me help push them out of your way. I wish we could see what is in front of us."

Ma wearily said, "Yes, Pa. I can smell and hear them."

Herman unwisely muttered, "Can we catch one and eat it?" Fortunately for him, Pa was far too excited to hear his audacity, and if he had, he would have ignored it. It wasn't the words but the way he said them. In the old country, Pa would have smacked him hard enough that a bruise would remind Herman of his manners for several days.

They emerged from the swampy forest to climb a little hill. The corduroy road stretched past a farmstead with a barn, a large house on a small hill, fences, and a clanking and clicking windmill spinning slowly in the slight breeze. Herman stared at the windmill, wondering what it did and how it worked. The bright sun announced it was almost time to begin the spring farm work as it thawed the ground. The gentle wind brought the cattle smell, which Pa considered the sweetest perfume, from the imposing barn.

Other farms sat behind the first one. They were all similar, with the houses facing the road and other buildings behind them. The close houses reminded Pa of his home village. Each house had fields, barns, and pastures stretching behind them, although not everyone had a windmill. A small cluster of buildings in the center looked out of place. The corduroy road was the only road, passing through the little village and continuing as far as they could see. The family could hear and smell animals grazing by the different barns; some animals wore bells that tinkled with every step.

At the first house, a man stopped digging in a garden and introduced himself. His only hair was a white fringe, and his leathery skin boasted of years working in the sun. His mighty hands, despite arthritis deforming his fingers, immediately grasped Pa's hand. His nearly toothless smile looked like it wanted to stretch from ear to ear. His clothes didn't have patches but were already dirty from his labors. Pa could only stare at him, not knowing his language.

Oscar joyfully laughed and, in Pa's native language, repeated himself, "Welcome, brother. I think we came from the same place, and here we are! My name's 'Oscar Liechstein,' and everyone calls me 'Oscar.' Have you had anything to eat? Come in and rest awhile, and tell me your story. Could your wife make stew and biscuits for us? I miss it so much! Come, come quickly!"

Pa smiled as he remembered meeting Oscar. "Yes, Mr. Furnace, Oscar was one fine man. He made it easier for us. Without Oscar, I'd have nothing. I only hoped to find a little hut and work for someone like I had in the old country. I never thought I could have all this. I owe everything to Oscar. He was an old, thin, tall man when I met him. He always seemed to laugh and never met a stranger. Oscar was a very good man. Better than I'll ever be, that's for sure."

The furnace struggled to burn bark on the logs. The pleasant smell of kindling escaped into the room as the flickering and snapping flames made a comforting invitation to sit back, relax, and enjoy the evening. The kindling had ignited, but Pa wanted to enjoy his furnace.

"Hmm, it looks like you've indigestion with your meal, Mr. Furnace. I better stay longer to ensure it catches, or Ma will be madder than when Herman wrapped a frog in her dishcloth. You must keep your wits around that boy.

"I can pass the time with the next part of our story. Would you like to hear more?"

Mr. Furnace sent a few sparks up the chimney. Pa laughed, the fire's reflection twinkling in his eyes, "I guess that's how you say yes."

He shut the firebox door, sat on his block, and leaned on the wall. He watched the struggling coals briefly before contentedly hooking his thumbs in his suspenders. He cleared his throat and restarted, smiling at his memories as they unfolded.

"Ah yes, there is nothing like a big meal with loved ones and good memories."

2

THE FARM

OSCAR HAD NEITHER CHILDREN NOR KINFOLK AND WAS A WIDOWER. HE hired Pa on the first day, letting the little family stay in the largest pig sty. It wasn't fancy but was dry and kept the winter wind out. This sty was twice the size of the other stys, big enough that Pa could stand straight up. They slept on the floor until Oscar insisted on them making feather beds from, of all the luxuries, woolen bags stuffed with wool.

Pigs don't like to dirty their living areas, so it was easy for Ma to sweep the wood floor clean, which was several inches higher than the ground. Ma immediately sensed that the higher floor kept the rainwater from puddling inside. The door fit tightly in the jam, although the family kept it open except during rainy or cold weather.

"Pa, this man's pigs have better homes than we had in the Old Country!" Ma could not get over their fortune.

Oscar hired Ma to cook and Edith to clean. Oscar owned 320 acres, about half in woods filled with mammoth oak trees. These trees were the straightest and tallest in the area and were in demand for different buildings. They raised corn and wheat on about 80 acres and alfalfa on the rest, except for a few acres of oats for the chickens. Crops exploded in the rich soil, overfilling Oscar's barn. About a third of the alfalfa was pasture, and Oscar harvested the rest to feed the stock during the harsh winter. Oscar believed in cows, pigs, chickens, and sheep. They pastored the animals during the summer but confined them in barns bigger than the Barron's castle during the winter. The cows made so much milk that they fed the excess to the pigs. There were enough chickens for everyone to have eggs daily; Mae wouldn't let anyone else care for them. She still frustrated Edith by petting the birds, which followed Mae around.

Oscar talked with Pa about wages the day after the family arrived. Each man would make one dollar per day, and Ma half that. Pa made sure to keep his family's wages.

"Ma, could you ever imagine how much Oscar is paying us?"

Ma smiled, "The Lord has brought us to a kind and generous man. We are so blessed."

Pa decided against commenting on how they stumbled onto their fortune.

The family could work in Oscar's garden and stay in the sty in return for vegetables. Edith's wages were supplies, including milk, eggs, salt, and meat. Usually, Oscar insisted the family ate meals with him in his house. Pa rigged a small mud chimney opposite the door to turn their sty into a cozy refuge, far more comfortable than their old shack. Edith particularly liked their coal oil lantern. Pa could buy enough fuel at the local supply store to use the lantern whenever they wanted. Edith always wanted to be the one to light it and then turn it out as they went to sleep.

"Ma, we never had so much money as what Oscar pays us. I can't get over our good fortune." Pa thought about what to do with his new riches continually.

"These walls fit together so tightly the wind can't get in, and you don't spend time putting mud on the outside as you did for our old shack. I like the wooden roof instead of the thatch one. Bugs, mice, and snakes don't fall on us while we sleep. The fireplace gives plenty of heat, making this little cabin our exotic getaway." Ma felt favored by their little house and everything in their new life.

The two-story house was huge, with high ceilings and glass windows. It had two ancient bot-bellied stoves, one in the dining room and one in the parlor, that struggled to heat the house. Ceiling registers let a little heat into the upstairs bedrooms. Each window and door had transits, providing natural circulation for summer cooling. Ma never ceased to be amazed by the curtains and each bedroom's closet. There were eight bedrooms, a dining room, a kitchen, a parlor (that the little family didn't know what it was for), a pantry, and a laundry room that opened to the back. The individual rooms were more extravagant than any of the rooms in the Barron's castle, at least, that Pa or Ma had seen. Under one corner of the house was a small root cellar with a heavy outside door. A covered porch circled the house and was the perfect place to sit in the evening and visit. Oscar's father had built the house, vainly hoping that Oscar would have a big family.

Many townspeople stopped by after supper, especially after finishing the spring planting and before fall harvesting began. Each brought news, gossip, or complaints about the weather or crops or to only sit and watch the sunset across the corduroy road. The little hill made the view more spectacular and usually led to arguments about the next few day's weather. Pa noticed that Oscar's home was the village social hub and decided it was because of his generosity with coffee and pie. Slowly, the family began learning the new language.

They got clean water from the windmill for washing, cooking, and drinking. Ma discovered the virtue of cleanliness and badgered her family to bathe. Pa didn't like it, but after Ma started warming bath water by their fireplace, Pa tolerated his Saturday night bath. Secretly, he thought, *my family does smell better since we began washing more.* Pa never hinted that bathing was a good idea and fussed about it every Saturday until he died. Pa took his bath first, then Ma, then each child in their birth order, reusing the same water. Ma rigged a blanket for bath privacy, another unexpected luxury.

Horses used a clever arrangement of pullies and cables to lift hay into the second-story barn mow, walking from the barn to the house across the large yard. Workers jammed wooden tines into the alfalfa on a wagon, and then, one horse raised the hay. Once in the air, another set of pulleys allowed a second horse to pull the alfalfa sideways into storage. It was backbreaking, dusty work, and Oscar always hired neighbors to help. Pa was amazed at the contraption when Oscar showed him how to work it. Oscar and the others also worked for neighbors when it was time to harvest their alfalfa.

The back of the barn opened to several fenced pastures. Cattle grazed freely in one, along with several draft horses. A skittish carriage horse usually stayed out of sight. The sheep grazed in another pasture, and the pigs grazed in a third. The pigs had tiny houses or sty spaced every few feet, while the sheep had a long, low building they could enter to avoid weather. The pasture fences made it more difficult for wild animals to chase the farm animals.

"Oscar, why do the sheep eat their pasture so close to the roots? They would have more food if they left it a little longer so the grass could grow better."

"One thing I have learned is sheep are something else. If one starts running, the others will quickly follow. They do the most foolish things. I had a blind one a few years ago. The other sheep followed that blind animal everywhere it went. It might get stuck in a corner, and the others packed around it. They had no idea what they were doing; they were following their blind leader. They would die of starvation if I hadn't done something. I wound up butchering the blind leader. It was not all that tasty, but what should I have done?"

The sty closest to the road was where the family lived. Oscar showed Pa how to build an outhouse, another unexpected luxury. Oscar made sure it was downwind from the sty, although odors from the farm animals always drifted into their tiny home. Pa enjoyed the smells as they reminded him how much his fortunes had changed since arriving. Mae always wrinkled her nose when the wind shifted, bringing the barn scents her way. She knew better than to say anything.

A long, narrow chicken coop with three rooms flanked the house, with one end opening into a fenced area. The chickens scratched under apple and pear trees, entering the coop at night to rest on horizontal poles in the first room. The center room held nesting boxes for the hens. Mae loved peeking into the boxes and collecting eggs, leaving some to hatch into chicks. Once, Herman found her carrying a chick in her pocket and never stopped teasing her. Oscar stored sacks of chicken feed in the last room, a mixture of finely ground corn and oats.

The fruit trees produced more fruit than everyone wanted. Oscar taught Ma how to can apples and pears. The young girls picked apples from the ground and fed the pigs what they didn't need. Oscar always had sugar, and Ma soon learned to bake pies, although it was hard work baking on the pot-bellied stove. Oscar had a heavy metal hood that Ma could put over the pie as it cooked. It was always in the way, but somehow, Ma managed to make the best pies. Everyone's mood improved when they walked into the house and breathed deeply the smell of a cooking cherry or apple pie.

In one corner were several walnut trees and three cherry trees. Everyone looked forward to ripe cherries, or rather, cherry pies, jams, and jellies. They fed wormy walnuts to the hogs, throwing the thick walnut skins into the pasture. They welcomed the remaining "good" nuts at their "end of the year" feast.

A large barn behind the orchard stored most of Oscar's harvest. The corn would be shocked, stalks tied into bundles and leaned against each other. Later, in the winter, Oscar's draft horses pulled a sled through the fields while the men loaded the shocks and brought them to the buildings where the family spent the winter days husking corn. Oscar had a special glove with nails in the palms to make the husking easier. He used the residue for animal bedding and had a mechanical tool to shell corn from the cob. A worker turned a wheel while feeding the cobs into a hole in the top. The kernels magically poured into a basket on one end while the cob popped out another chute. A child could shell more corn in an hour than a man could do all day by hand. Pa could only stare at it with his mouth open the first time he saw it work. There was a large storage bin for wheat, another for corn, and a couple more for unknown purposes.

Oscar used most of his grain to feed his farm animals, selling the surplus in a nearby city. He used the money to pay taxes and buy things he couldn't make.

The mow was above the cattle and horses, making it easy to feed alfalfa to the animals. The main barn was huge, thirty feet high, and several hundred feet long. There was a horse pen, a cattle pen, a separate place to milk cows, and a place to store tillage equipment or wagons in the center. Hand-hewn beams, held together by wooden pegs instead of tied with worn ropes, framed the sturdy barn. The siding was large, rough-cut cottonwood planks pushed tightly together. Oscar believed that making the barn comfortable for people made it comfortable for the animals, and comfortable cows gave more milk.

A smaller lean-to shed on one side of the barn held a plow, tillage tools, and other equipment. Oscar had several wagons in addition to the sled and carriage. Along the walls were neat rows of hand tools, such as scythes, sickles, axes, sledgehammers, and saws. Oscar hung different-sized traps from the rafters, some for small animals like rabbits and others for larger animals like wolves.

"I set traps for the varmints in the winter. The meat is good, the hides are warm, and it helps keep them from eating my crops and livestock." Oscar loved talking about his operation.

"You ever get anything larger, like bears or deer?" Pa had heard of bears and wasn't sure he ever wanted to see one.

"Well, we don't have bear in these parts. There are a few deer, but they don't seem to get in my traps. So far, they leave me alone, so I leave them alone, except sometimes I've hunted them in winter. I've caught possums, a few raccoons, and twice a skunk. I don't want any more skunks. I didn't mind the smell, but my wife did. I feared she'd make me sleep in the barn until I died. Do you know you can't wash that stink off? It must wear off, which takes a long time. I got used to it, but she never did, not to the day she passed." Oscar shook his head sadly at his memories.

Near the house, by the windmill, was Oscar's garden, where he grew vegetables and potatoes. Pa's family expanded and cared for the garden, and because Oscar generously shared his bounty, they never went hungry again. Oscar sold the produce they could not use, making him one of the few farmers who regularly traveled to the city.

All the roofs were rough planks covered with shake shingles. "Every few years, some fellow comes around with a machine that carves shingles. His price is right, and we always need more. I know he's coming and have trees felled and squared, ready. Truth be known, I think he needs the money, and I'm glad to help him out." Oscar always planned and yet was generous at the same time. Pa was curious about what this carving machine looked like.

Oscar insisted that the little family attend church on Sunday. Pa was wise enough to comply, although he spent his worship time daydreaming, interrupted only to stand or to sit. It was hard since he knew so little of the language.

After finishing the other chores in winter, Oscar always cut a few trees for lumber, dragging trees to a sawmill in the next town. "You never know when you must build or repair a coop, fence, or something."

Oscar taught Pa how to farm in this new land. Shearing the sheep was early on the spring list. Pa had never worked with sheep, but Oscar showed him how to use the shears and then bag and tie the wool in burlap. Pa compensated for his lack of skill by holding the sheep with his mighty strength. Once satisfied Pa could do it, Oscar disappeared while Pa finished the job. He soon reappeared with a neighbor lady in tow, a middle-aged, stern woman. The woman showed Ma how to cord the wool, spin it to a thread, and tie it into long rolls. When the weaver came to town, Ma gave him the wool thread, which he magically changed into rough cloth.

"Pa, having new cloth for clothes instead of the Barron's castoffs is more than I could ever have hoped for," Ma exclaimed one night. "We can make clothes without holes and aren't so thin we can almost see through them."

Pa knew how to use a mule or wooden shovels in the Old Country for field preparation. Now, Oscar taught Pa how to use the heavy draft horses. Pa's massive strength made him a natural with the giants. Pa never stopped being amazed at the ease with which these behemoths pulled metal plows and how much they ate. He never missed his mule's stubbornness. "The Barron never gave us metal plows or shovels to make our jobs easier," Pa muttered.

Oscar butchered a cow or a pig as soon as it turned cold. He had an old tree where he hung the carcass to cool for a few days. Near the chicken house was a small smokehouse with a concrete floor. Oscar showed Pa how to cut and hang the meat in the smokehouse. They built a small fire and tightly shut the smokehouse. Once the smoke stopped billowing from the little vent on top, they opened the building and restarted the fire. Eventually, Oscar decided the meat was ready to be cut into chunks for tight packing into one-gallon crock pots. They melted suet and poured a fat seal over the beef before setting the crocks into the snow to cool. Later, they moved them to the root cellar.

"Pa, did you know you could store meat like this?" Ma was curious.

"No. I wonder if the Barron did. If so, he never told the rest of us. We used to take turns butchering our animals. Each family got a portion, so we didn't store any. Oscar said the crocks will last through summer until the chickens have grown enough for the table. This system is so much better. I think we wasted a lot the other way. Oscar's system uses almost all the meat."

One week before Christmas, Oscar found Pa and asked him to help with a chore. The two men got a saw and walked to a clump of small pine trees. Only a tiny dusting of early snow was on the ground, not even enough to cover the alfalfa. The sharp wind promised cold weather for the future. Oscar looked at the different trees, rejecting one after another, straining Pa's patience. Finally, he decided that one tree, about five feet high, met his exacting standards. Pa cut the tree with the saw, and they carried it back to the buildings.

Oscar made Pa recut the bottom of the tree, but this time, instructed him to be sure the cut was square with the trunk. While Pa finished, Oscar disappeared, returning with a large washtub full of rocks and two short boards. They nailed the boards to the bottom of the tree and carried everything into the parlor. Oscar set the tree into the washtub and covered the boards with the rocks.

"Edith, please get enough water to cover the rocks." Oscar requested.

Several times every day, Oscar had Edith add more water to the wash tub. The thirsty tree drank increasing amounts of water as it warmed.

"Pa, it is Christmas Eve. We will rest this afternoon. I'll ask Ma to fix us a feast fit for a king. Come over a little early for supper, will you?" Oscar's eyes twinkled, adding a mischievous look to his ever-present smile.

The family gathered for supper and enjoyed the best feast Pa could remember. The family laughed and talked, but Oscar only watched and smiled. Later, Pa commented that he had enjoyed himself more than the others.

Once supper was over, Oscar herded everyone into the Parlor. "Edith, would you go upstairs into the end room and bring the box in the closet."

Edith brought the box, and Oscar opened it. "Here, Mae, you start hanging these onto the tree. Spread them out, yes, like that. Good. Herman, you can put this angel on the very top of the tree."

Herman took the most beautiful doll he had ever seen and carefully placed it on top of the tree.

"Ma, look how the glass ornaments reflect the candles. They are so beautiful."

Oscar laughed. "Yes, they are. We are celebrating Jesus, our Savior's birth. Now, Edith, open that cabinet. There should be a small cloth on top. Yes, that is the one. Spread the cloth over the cabinet top. Next, there should be a little barn. That's it. Jesus was born in a cattle barn. It's hard to believe that the ruler of the universe was born that way, but He was.

"Now, put the feed trough inside the barn. Do you see the little babe? Put Him in the manger. His mother and father go on either side. His father isn't his natural father; the Bible says that the Holy Spirit overshadowed Mary, His mother.

"This is an exciting time, so kings from the East come to pay homage to the Savior. Put them there. An angel announces the birth, so hang that angel from the little nail on the barn's roof. Do you see it?

"If something like an angel fills the sky, people will want to know what is happening. Put the shepherds and their sheep over on the one side. They came to see what all the excitement was about."

Everyone looked at the little manger scene, drinking in Oscar's story.

"Now, Luis, Please go into my bedroom and get those packages under the bed. Thank you."

As Oscar handed each child a package, they respectfully thanked him. Luis opened his present to find a new rifle. Herman discovered a book. Edith admired a fancy plate, and Mae hugged her new doll. Ma opened her package to find a comb and brush, while Pa opened his package to enjoy a pair of work gloves. Oscar could hardly stop laughing from his joy.

Then Oscar reached behind a chair to get a large sack. He gave each of them an orange.

"Ma, what is this?" Mae asked.

Oscar laughed even more. "It is called an orange. First, you peel the cover. Then, you carefully take one slice. You start eating it by sucking the juice, then the pulp. Be sure not to eat the seeds. Watch."

"Oh, it is so sweet!" Exclaimed Edith.

About that time, there was a knock on the door. Oscar jumped up and found the village children on his porch. The children began singing

Christmas songs as the family crowded around the door. Pa didn't know what they were until later. After the children finished, Oscar gave each one an orange.

"Ma, may I do that next year? Mae asked.

"We will see," Ma replied. "You have to learn the songs first."

"It is time for us to go to vespers. Grab the lanterns and foot warmers." Oscar said.

The foot warmers were metal tins they shoveled coals from the stove into. The family and Oscar walked to the church. Oscar and Pa sat on the men's side with the other men, and Ma sat on the women's side. The four children sat in the center, alert to whatever would happen. The church was decorated with many candles and filled with villagers.

The preacher told the Christmas story, and the congregation sang songs. Finally, the preacher blessed them, and everyone left for the night.

It snowed so much that a drift completely blocked the sty's door that night. Oscar brought a shovel and dug a path from the door.

"What are those things on your feet?" Asked Pa.

"They are snow shoes. Here, I brought another pair for you. They allow me to walk on top of the snow. We can make more for the rest of your family. The people who used to live here invented them, and one showed me how to make them."

The only work Oscar allowed was feeding the animals on Christmas day. They sat in the big house and talked about the things that friends talk about, which was everything and nothing. The family often remembered how pleasant that first Christmas was.

Pa always reflected on how much Oscar did for them. The little family worked hard, and Oscar's farm prospered more this year than in years. Fortunately, Oscar knew their native language, was well-liked in the nearby town, and introduced Pa to everyone.

"Ma, Oscar has more ways to make work easier than I ever thought. It's no wonder he is so prosperous."

"I can't believe he pays us so much. We are truly blessed, Pa. We have good cloth for decent clothes, good boots for cold weather, and a warm place to sleep. What more could we ask for?"

In late spring, the family heard the sounds of pans clinking from the corduroy road. Ma looked out the window to see a short, stocky man with pots and pans tied all over his body. He had a big soup pot for a hat and a bag slung over his shoulder. He strolled as if weighted by the cares of the world. Instead, it was the weight of all his utensils. Every step rattled his wares, a discordant symphony.

Pa and Ma went to the road to talk with this unusual visitor.

"Hello, friends. I am John Witherson, descended from the noble Witherson clan in Boston. My family has a smything tradition. I repair pots and small tools, sell household goods like needles, and fix small farm equipment. Can I interest you in any of my wares? Perhaps a fine frying pan made in the style of ancient Egyptian pharaohs? Needles for sewing shirts and repairing saddles are my specialty."

The tinker liked big words and talked in a pompous fashion. His big beard made him look important, although his mustache was smaller than Pa's.

Oscar joined them. "Well, Mr. Tinker. I broke my harness needle, and I need a new one. How much for your best?"

"It is cheap at my price, merely a small, pitiful coin and a meal."

Oscar turned to Ma. "Set another plate for our guest."

The tinker liked talking and told tales of faraway adventures, including fantastic beasts that hunted on land and in the water, cooking their food with hot breath, and stealing fishermen's livelihood. He claimed pirates abducted him and found lost treasure that the bandits kept for themselves. He had made friends with a colony of talking bears, with whom he hibernated during one particularly nasty winter. That was hard, he proclaimed, since bears get grouchy if woke, and he had to be careful when he got up to relieve himself.

Ma and Pa had trouble understanding the stories but gathered the basics. Oscar encouraged the tinker, commenting in amazement at the tales, each more surprising than the last. Finally, the tinker rummaged in his oily sack and pulled out a handful of needles wrapped in a tattered rag. Oscar selected one large needle and paid the asking price.

"Thank you, kind sir. The meal was one of the best I have had. It was fit for kings and emperors. But I need to be on my way."

While whistling an unfamiliar tune, the tinker adjusted his wares before finding his way to the road. It wasn't long before the banging pot sounds drifted into the distance.

Pa looked at Oscar, "I thought I saw a harness needle on that shelf by the saddles. Why did you need another?"

Oscar smiled, "A tinker is a wretched and lonely man. He lives by selling things no one needs. Usually, their families have either died or want nothing to do with them. Most people curse him or sic their dogs on them when one stops by. They have the reputation, probably undeserved, of being thieves. They wander from village to village, hoping for a speck of kindness. Tinkers become tinkers when they have nothing else they can do except starve. They make up entertaining adventures and put on a happy face, all hoping for a bread crust. They pay for their food with an entertaining story or two. The Bible says to open your house to people like them because you might entertain an angel."

"I hope angels smell better than that guy. His stories are nothing but lies and foolishness. Oscar, I hope he did not take you in." Ma was a little on the angry side.

"No, I knew everything he said was meant to impress us. He is such a failure in life that he needed us to think he is important. We usually get a tinker every few years. Did you notice how worn his shoes were and how patched his clothes were? It cost me so little to be nice, and you must admit that he was entertaining. We must get to work, for we have burned enough daylight." With that, Oscar led the men to the fields.

Later, Ma talked to Pa about the tinker. "I have been thinking about that tinker. Oscar was nice to him and also to us. We must remember that we could be roaming the world searching for food scraps. I feel terrible for being so harsh."

Pa paused before replying, "Perhaps we can do better next time. After all, Oscar has taken care of us. I feel like he has made us his family."

A gentle, soothing drizzle began falling. Pa's snoring punctuated the quiet sounds of rain. All the children except Herman fell asleep. His mind raced as he thought how exciting it must be to roam the countryside talking to various people.

But, in the changing frontier, that was the last tinker to walk the Corduroy road.

One day, a stranger found Pa working in the barn. "I am the local church's pastor. I want to teach your children to read, write, and do arithmetic. I meet with several other students on Sunday afternoons. Will you let them come?"

"Can Ma and I come as well?"

"Of course. We meet at the church. You can walk there. Our classroom isn't much, but it'll do."

"If Oscar says it's okay, we will come."

Later, Pa discovered Oscar had suggested it. Pa barely learned his letters but did learn enough to be able to read bills and receipts. Luis' bad attitude hindered his learning. Ma didn't struggle with the lessons. Edith was the star, and she usually helped the rest with their studies, although once Herman buckled down, he did the best of all.

Then, on Christmas of their third year, Oscar approached Pa.

"I don't have children nor close relatives. I want to sell you my property. You've taken good care of it, and you have a fine family. You'll respect the land, unlike some of these other young'uns. Don't worry about the money; I'll hold the note. I only ask that I live in the house."

It was a good deal, and Pa accepted it. He had become a landowner, just like the Barron, except without serfs. Ever since that Christmas, Pa worked harder but often strutted around the barnyard like a young rooster, head back, surveying his tiny empire. He became more demanding of his family. It seemed that nothing anyone could do was good enough. The stew tasted differently, the boys didn't milk the cows properly, and the chickens weren't eating enough bugs. Pa didn't notice how his family, especially Edith, avoided him when they could.

Oscar visited the supply store three weeks after filing the deed's paperwork. He suddenly clutched his chest, bent over, and slowly rolled to the ground with a sickening thump. As he drew his knees to his chest, he moaned a deep, lonesome moan. Men ran to get the preacher, but Oscar was gone before his arrival.

They held Oscar's funeral in his parlor. The parlor was the "fancy room" of the house, where Oscar received the preacher or the town mayor and hardly ever used for any other purpose. It was the largest room and had a bay window. Oscar, like the other farmers, kept his best furniture here. The chairs even had cushions. The parlor was central to the house and heated by a large pot-bellied stove with ceiling registers, allowing heat to circulate to the upper floor.

The bay window was huge, almost from floor to ceiling, taking up half the outside wall. A strategic door to the outdoor porch made setting a casket in front of the windows easy. The preacher placed a cloth with church symbols on a wooden stand in front of the window before the pallbearers brought the coffin in. Pa had never asked what they used this room for, but now he could see how practical it was for funerals. It was the first one in the little village since the family arrived.

Everyone attended Oscar's funeral, overflowing the parlor and filling adjoining rooms. Children either stood or sat on the floor quietly. Most people soon took their outer coats off, giving them to children to carry into a bedroom. The men either stood or sat stoically, but many women silently cried. Children old enough to understand clung tightly to their mothers.

After the preacher opened in prayer, most attendees stood and said nice things about Oscar, summarizing their emotions.

"He was always cheery."

"He helped everyone with any needs."

"I never saw a man that good with the children."

"Why was he so generous?"

The adults nodded assent with each comment. Finally, the preacher gave his message.

"It's hard for me to add much to Oscar's memory. You have all experienced how he lived his faith, taking it very seriously. He frequently came by and prayed with me, and I know he helped many widows. Most of us don't know everything he did for people. Heaven gained a saint, but we'll miss our departed saint."

It was late before everyone finally went home. Pa stayed to talk with the preacher.

"Oscar was special to me and my family. The ground's frozen, but I want to dig his grave. Show me where, and I'll start in the morning. My boys and I will bring the coffin then."

Pa dug Oscar's grave the next day, breaking through the frozen soil with a pickax. While Pa worked, Luis and Herman brought the horses and wagon back to the farm and returned to the waiting chores. Pa's job was backbreaking and slow until he dug below the frozen dirt. Shortly, Pa took his coat off, sweat dripping and freezing onto his collar. Finally, he finished, and the preacher and Pa lowered the pine box. Pa filled the hole while the preacher carefully pounded a rough cross with Oscar's name painted on it, said a prayer, and the two men went home.

The next day, the government clerk, Joe Losten, strutted onto the farm. He was the part-time town clerk and the local banker. Today, he was on official business. Pa stared him down as Joe walked to the barn.

"I have good news for you. Today, I am executing Oscar's will. He forgave your note and left enough money to pay taxes and buy spring supplies. It looks like you're debt-free. Congratulations!"

The family moved into the big farmhouse. The parents had a first-floor room, and each excited child had their second-floor room. Mae insisted on having the room facing the chicken coop, allowing her to watch the chickens scratch for bugs before bedtime. It was cold upstairs because the two pot-bellied stoves barely heated the upstairs rooms. Still, Oscar had many comforters and feather beds – soft wool, unlike the course burlap they had in the old country - allowing everyone to snuggle deep for warmth. They still wore their wolf-skin hats in winter.

It was a full moon on their first night in their new house, the temperature dropping in the cloudless sky. The snow stopped falling, and the air stirred slightly. Although they needed foot warmers, they didn't need each other's body heat to stay warm. Luis could not believe their new luxuries.

The rising full moon streamed light through the dormant fruit trees, casting eerie shadows looking like long, dancing fingers on walls. They had just put their lanterns out when Herman quietly slipped into Mae's room.

"Mae! *I saw him.*"

"Who?"

"The ghost chicken! It ran through the yard!"

"You did not see any such thing! Go to bed! *There's no such thing.*" She paused, covering her mouth with her hand, "Is there?"

"I don't know. All I know is what I saw. You remember that one, a couple of days ago, that somehow got loose and ran away after we cut its head off?"

"It slipped from Luis' hands." Mae's voice quivered as she tightly gripped the comforter to her chin.

"Yes, but we never found it, did we?"

"A, A, A dog or a coyote got it."

"I don't know. Maybe it's mad at us. Maybe it's looking for its head. *Maybe it wants one of ours.* Maybe…. Listen."

The wind blew gently through a tree, making a quiet, low moan. At the same time, a branch bumped something as the wind moved the branch shadows on the walls.

"I think you're right. It's nothing. I'm going back to my room. Good night."

"Herman, you scared me. *Don't leave me alone.*"

But Herman was gone.

Mae jumped from her covers and ran into Edith's room.

"Edith, Herman says there's a ghost chicken outside. What'll we do?"

"Huh, what?" Edith groggily opened her eyes.

"Can I sleep here tonight?"

"You can't believe what Herman says."

"I'm too scared to sleep."

"You're too old to let something so foolish scare you."

Edith made room for Mae to climb into her bed and promptly fell asleep. Mae, conversely, cowered under the covers before finally succumbing to a fitful, nightmare-filled sleep, chased by ghost chickens.

Ma never understood why Mae became so afraid of the chickens after they moved into the house. She still cared for them but was very careful to do her work during daylight and became fearful when entering the coop. Sometimes, she insisted with tears that her mother go with her. When asked, Mae wouldn't say what happened.

Pa stopped at the supply store after finishing his noon chores. "Hello, Orney. How are things in these parts today?"

Orney looked up from a flyer. "Hello, neighbor. I have an opportunity for you. Your place has some of the biggest and straightest oak trees around. Here is a timber order. Are you interested?"

Pa didn't have to think long. "Yes. What do you need?"

The two men closed the deal, and Pa returned to the farm.

The next day, the men gathered their tools and headed to the woods. Herman and Luis cut several oak trees with the crosscut saw while Pa used his ax to trim branches. They then cut the limbs into smaller lengths to feed their stoves. They returned for the logs once they brought the sled to the buildings.

Now, the men began the heavy work. They hitched the horses to the logs to pull them back to the buildings. Pa started on the first log while the boys returned for the others. After bringing the trees to the barnyard, the boys returned with several sled loads of firewood made from the branches. Pa had discovered it was easier dragging logs than trees covered in branches.

Pa got his broad ax and a short-handled sledgehammer from his tool shed. The broad ax had a short handle, less than two feet long, and a wide blade with a tip curving slightly to the right. A post opposite the edge was made to be hit by a heavy sledgehammer. Pa manhandled the broad ax with his left hand while swinging the sledgehammer with his right. Standing on the log, he "carved" giant slivers of wood, changing the round tree into a square beam, each sledgehammer blow echoing off the buildings. It was exhausting work, and even the best woodsman could only do it for an hour before resting. However, Pa never needed rest and, having a natural skill, quickly carved the logs into fourteen-inch square timber. Rumor was the foundation beams were for a railroad station. The girls collected the slivers, which were the perfect length for the pot-bellied stoves, and stacked them in the wood pile.

Orney asked Pa to make several beams and smaller crossties eight inches square and eight feet long. They needed the beams immediately and the crossties in a few months. He had to deliver the smaller ones, cut to length, to the supply store. Pa considered the work a good use of their otherwise winter's idle time.

The two boys finished dragging logs just before dark and, without instructions, began chores. They stabled the horses, brushed and wiped them down before throwing heavy wool blankets on them. Luis climbed into the mow and threw food for the horses and the cows into their respective mangers. Herman started milking cows while Luis threw the windmill lever to pump water for the animals' troughs. Oscar had devised a clever pipe system to fill all the water troughs, saving the effort of carrying many gallons of water.

Both boys knew better than to get near the chicken coop. Mae always threw a royal fit if she saw them near "her" chickens. They didn't care because Mae happily collected the eggs, changed the water, and fed the birds. At least she used to do it cheerfully, but now she was more apprehensive. Herman noticed Mae's attitude change but didn't know what to do about it. He did not dare tell anyone of his little joke, fearing his father's wrath.

Finally, the two young men finished the chores and returned to the house. Supper was especially welcome after the day's hard work. Pa put his tools away on his way to the barn. Once inside, he affectionately patted the draft horses' giant heads and smiled as they shook their massive manes. He glanced at the full mows, feeling his prosperity deep in his soul. *Life is good,* Pa decided.

"Boys, I am so glad we can work together. You make our lives so much easier." Pa gave his horses a good night pat, ensured they were comfortable, and closed his barn doors.

Pa jauntily marched towards the house, not knowing what he was heading into.

3
The Fight

A starving Pa made a grand entrance into the dining room, sat at the table, and surveyed his children. Luis was growing into a big man, looking like he could successfully wrestle wild bears, the result of more and better food than in the old country. Herman was the tallest and the most scholarly. Edith became a fine young woman, soon ready for marriage. Mae had settled down and applied herself to growing up. Prosperity had erased most of Ma's haggardness, and now she bustled with renewed energy. Pa's pride in his family and how well they adapted to their new country swelled in his chest. *They all work hard, every one of them. I am so lucky to have my wife, daughters, and sons. They help the farm prosper.* Hardly a day passed when he didn't congratulate himself on his decision to flee his country, and today was no different.

Now, there were four more, three little boys and a tiny girl barely two months old. The girl had a terrible cough, and Ma held her close. *It won't be long, and the little boys will be able to start working the fields.* Pa eagerly anticipated putting more field hands to good use.

Ma stirred stew simmering on the decrepit, potbellied stove using her spare hand. Herman retrieved an armload of wood while Luis struggled with his reader. He knew better than to argue with Pa. Pa instinctively knew education was critical in their new land, as was speaking the new language.

Edith walked to her father. "Would you like to practice the language?"

Pa nodded. The new language was challenging for him, yet he stubbornly persisted. He hated that Ma understood it with seemingly less effort, as if she was born knowing it. He usually did well until he got angry, which he often did. He never did learn the new curse words; instead, he switched to his old language. His children knew those words meant "time to hide."

He couldn't admit he was jealous of his wife. The church ladies immediately adopted her, and the women gathered weekly. One day, they were canning vegetables, meat, preserves, and even root beer; the next week, they made quilts, and the week after, clothing. They rotated working at each other's houses, which was more of an opportunity for socializing than production. Their constant chatter gave Pa a headache, and he always found something to do elsewhere when they came, even in torrential rain. But, he admitted, they also taught Ma how to manage things in the home and helped her with the language. He had no time to visit with other farmers and didn't want to anyway.

No one could ever break Pa's iron rules. His word was absolute law, never questioned nor debated, and his temper grew with his prosperity. Everyone worked hard. Friends could visit but only talk in the parlor and only after they finished their work. They must only speak their new language.

This last rule caused him the most grief. Pa often forgot the word for something, reducing him to unceremonious pointing. While working, he often told Luis, "Get me, get me, get me that thing from the shed!" Woe to Luis if he didn't come back with the right thing. Pa never did well when even slightly humiliated.

Ma adjusted the kettle slightly, causing part of the old, rusty stove top to collapse into the fire and release a smelly cloud of smoke. Everyone started coughing, and the baby screamed louder. While bouncing the child, Ma unsuccessfully tried using the pot to plug the hole. Edith jumped to take the child while Mae grabbed a frying pan, which covered the gaping hole better.

"Pa, this old potbellied stove is plum *worn* out. It needs replacing. It's older than dirt, even older than we are!"

"Now, Ma…"

"*Don't 'now Ma' me!'* The other one is in even worse condition. You know we need new ones, and we can't make a decent fire, and we're all cold. It is winter, and you look at us! Everyone has runny noses, and the baby hasn't stopped crying. I think it might have pneumonia or consumption or *something*."

"Ma, we've been through much worse."

"Maybe, but we don't have to live like this! It is harder to heat this house than the old hut. You need to do something about it before we all get sick and die a horrible death!"

"Enough!" Pa slammed his massive fist onto the table, bouncing plates and cups, raising a cloud of soot, and rattling Mae's fork to the floor. None of the children exhaled, all staring intently at their plates, while the baby screamed even louder.

Ma wasn't stopping. "You keep bragging about how good the crops were. Each of our cows had fine calves, and the chickens are doing better than anyone could expect. Look, you're even selling those beams to the railroad people. We can get a new stove that doesn't choke us at every turn."

"I'll go to town tomorrow and see if the supply store can get us a new top."

"A new top! What about the rest of it? *It's all worn out.* The stove pipe rusted through, and the bin spills ash to the floor. It's a wonder it hasn't set the house on fire. Everything is filthy, our clothes are filthy, and this ash makes everyone itch. I think Oscar's father installed this stove."

"That's enough!"

"Well, are you going to do something or not? Don't be so mule-headed stubborn. You know what we need and can get a new one." The children had never seen anyone, least of all their mother, stand up to Pa like this.

Pa jumped to his feet, his roar sounding like a cross between an angry bull and a wounded bear, followed by words in his native language that he shouldn't have used. He flung his coat on and stomped out. Edith thought the door broke when he slammed it. No one said anything until little Mae sneezed, causing a puff of ash to float upward.

Ma brought the stew kettle to the table and served each child the now gritty gruel.

After they finished eating, Ma told Edith, "You take the rest of this stew to that stubborn husband of mine. Wait, take this large piece of his favorite pie. Can you carry his coffee as well? Don't forget your coat. And you listen. If you tell him I sent this to him, I'll spank you like you've never been spanked. You're not too old, you know. Tell him you snuck it from the stove. It must look like your idea. That stubborn man! He's a good man, just more stubborn than most mules!"

Edith brought supper to her father. He was sitting on a wood block, leaning against the barn siding, telling his troubles to his draft horses in his old language. They nibbled a little alfalfa before raising their immense heads, watching him as they chewed.

"Pa, I have some supper."

"Don't want any."

"But Pa, Ma said that if she caught me bringing it to you, I'd be in big trouble."

"Looks like you're in trouble."

"Pa, please! You worked hard today. Eat for me. I'll wait here while you do."

"Ma put you up to this, didn't she."

"Pa, the baby is so sick. I couldn't get it to stop crying. What'll we do?"

"I don't know. This problem is something I can't fix or run from." Pa reached for the stew, and suddenly it was gone. He never noticed eating it.

"Pa, was anyone else ever that sick?"

"No, Edith. No one. I don't understand. Here, I've finished the stew and coffee. There's a bite of pie left. Will you eat it?"

"OK. It's my favorite. Let me have the bowl and cup, and I'll go back in."

"I'm staying out here. I need to figure this out."

"Night, Pa." And Edith ran back to the house.

The children gathered in the dining room in the morning, but Ma was unusually late. Edith started cooking eggs and biscuits while the rest talked about childish things. In short, it was a typical morning. No one noticed the baby had stopped crying.

When she reached the dining room, Ma silently threw her coat over her night clothes and rushed to the barn. Pa was sleeping, still sitting on his block while leaning on a wall.

"Pa, wake up."

"Huh, Ma, what're you doing out here dressed like that?"

"Pa, the baby died last night."

Pa jumped up and sprinted to the house, followed by his wife. He burst into the dining room and wordlessly ran to his bedroom. Moments later, his children heard his wail.

The funeral was a day later. The tiny casket sat in the bay window, and the house filled with mourners again. Ma had cried her heart dry, but Pa only stared at the coffin. Soon, the service was over, and they carried the casket to a freshly dug hole in the village cemetery.

After they covered it, everyone went home except Edith and Pa, who stared at the newly covered grave. The winter snow started turning a dirty gray, awaiting the next snowfall. The wind's icy breath caused Edith to shiver, but Pa's fierce anger wouldn't let him notice the cold. He continued clenching and unclenching his fists while his beard and eyebrows appeared standing on end. His eyes had no luster, dulled from his pain.

"I'm so wrong, and I don't know what to do, Edith." Pa's voice was barely more than a whisper.

"Pa, it'll be okay."

"No, it won't. Not now, not ever. Well, I have a lot of work to do." And Edith watched him stride home, each step screaming volumes of fury. Pa was different from then on. He worked long hours by lantern like a madman, still sleeping in the barn and talking even less. Finally, he finished the beams and delivered the ties. The railroad paid in cash.

Ma had started attending Sunday services soon after Oscar sold them the house. Something about it drew her. She couldn't say whether it was the fellowship, the teaching, or the songs.

"Ma, why do you always go to the church? Your place is here, like mine." Pa was mildly annoyed.

"I like it. Will you come with me?"

Pa snorted in disgust. "I don't have time." And that ended all discussion about attending church.

The small church was about a half mile away on the corduroy road, tucked against the cemetery. Three sections of rough-hewn benches filled the room except for the relatively new pot-bellied stove. The front had a rough cross behind a crude table with a candle. Windows let sunlight in, and at night, the worshipers brought lanterns. The men sat on the right side, the women on the other, and the children in the center—woe to any child acting differently than their parents expected.

The preacher enthusiastically preached his sermons, tending to shout rather than speak.

Finally, one cold Sunday, curiosity conquered Pa, and after his family left, he walked to the church. He stood outside a window and listened. First, they sang songs telling of eternity. Pa had never thought about what happened after death. Then they prayed, asking for good things for everyone in the village, the nation, and even the world.

He doesn't know much of the world, like the Barron and his endless, useless wars, Pa thought to himself.

Then they prayed things he didn't understand, something about getting sins forgiven. His brow furrowed more. "What is sin?" he quietly muttered, unsure who he spoke to.

Next, the preacher read from a book. Based on the preacher's voice, that book was different and critical to the service. *Maybe it was the same book that Ma insisted on lugging everywhere during their flight.*

Finally, the preacher started talking.

"Do you know what's one of the biggest sins you and I and the world have? It's stubbornness. That's what it is. We are so stubborn! You can teach them, but mules must make up their mind. It's the same with us people. We're so stubborn. We can't back down no matter what, even when we know it is the right thing to do. We're so stubborn because of our pride. We think our word is law, and there can never be anything other than what we say! Some of you left the old country because of stubborn men. They were destroying themselves and everyone else because of their stubbornness.

"That's what it does. It destroys the weakest first and then moves on until no one's left. You must give your stubbornness to Jesus. He can take that stubbornness and nail it to the cross, kill it off forever, and replace it with His love."

Pa had heard enough and slunk home, his heavy boots crunching the frozen snow, his head hanging low, and his shoulders slumping. The pastor's words ate his conscience. *No one is weaker than my little girl was. What will I do next, destroy the rest of my family?*

Pa was waiting at the table when Ma returned and started making dinner.

"Did you have a good time at church?" Something in Pa's tone made her look up quickly.

"Yes, I did."

"Well, what happened?"

"We sang hymns, prayed, read the Bible, then the preacher preached."

"What did he preach on?

"He talked about stubborn rebellion and how it hurts those you love most. I see so many times I am so stubborn, and I know it hurts everyone. I asked God to forgive me and change me. He will."

"So, he told everyone I was stubborn, did he?"

"Oh no, he didn't! The preacher said we're all stubborn. Every one of us wants our way."

"You think I am stubborn?"

Ma turned, bent over her husband, and quickly kissed him on the forehead. Pa flinched at her unusual affection, especially in front of his family. "Pa, you're like everyone else, no different. You're special to me, but as far as stubbornness goes, you're nothing special. The preacher never even hinted anything about you. The only person he said was stubborn was himself and his mule."

No one said much else that day.

Early Monday, Ma didn't hear Pa leave, "Luis, where's Pa?"

"I don't know. Maybe in the barn? I'll check."

A few minutes later, he returned to the house. "Pa's not there, and all the horses are in their stalls. I need to go back to feed them."

"Don't worry, he'll show up. He's always strutting around somewhere, showing off, and thinking he's a big shot."

Pa walked to the church and waited outside until the preacher strolled to the church shortly after sunrise. "Pretty cold to be standing out here, friend. Let's go into the church and make the pot-bellied stove do its job.

"Now, what can I do for you on this early morning, my friend."

"I heard a little of your sermon Sunday. I'm very stubborn, and it cost my baby. What do I need to do?"

The preacher thought for a moment. "Well, the Bible says if you confess your sins, Jesus is faithful and just to forgive them."

"Okay, I just did that, and I'm the same." Pa gruffly replied.

"To receive forgiveness, you must know that Jesus is God and died on the cross for everything you did wrong. You must make him your Lord, believe God rose him from the dead, and confess Him to others. You have to trust Him."

"Is 'Lord' like the Barron in the old country?"

"Yes, only more so. He doesn't just ask you to work for Him; He also helps and changes you into who He wants you to be. Not only does He tell you what to do, but you must acknowledge everything comes from Him. And He does more. He becomes your best friend. Some call Him 'the Lover of Your Soul'"

"How can I do that? Take the beams I just delivered to the railroad. I did the work, not God."

"Yes, but God gave you the opportunity. He made you strong, grew the trees, and even directed the railroad to you."

"How do I do I make him Lord?"

"By prayer. You only tell Him what He already knows, that you're consumed with doing wrong. Then, you give control of your life to Jesus. He does the rest. Somehow, He changes us if only we let Him."

"I don't know."

"Friend, please don't be stubborn. It's too important."

"What about my baby?"

"I don't know about your baby. The rest of your family has made Jesus their Lord."

"I noticed they changed. Herman isn't teasing Mae like he used to. But my baby, what about her?"

"You see, friend, if Jesus is your Lord, He collects your soul to be with Him after you die. Souls not collected go straight to torment in the horrible fires of Hell."

"You telling me my baby is burning in Hell? *Is that it*? Because I am so stubborn?"

"Sit down, friend, sit down. God's a good God. He cares about your baby just like He cares about you."

"She was only a couple of months old! She didn't even know her own name!"

"Friend, we can't do anything about the past. But we can do something about the present and the future."

"I am the reason she died. I should go to Hell, not her!" Pa stared at the intense fire burning brightly in the stove and shuddered.

"Friend, that's true. There's nothing you can do not to go there. But Jesus loves you too much for that to happen – if you believe and trust Him."

The dam holding back Pa's tears broke. The preacher put his hand on Pa's back. "Friend, please, don't let your baby girl have died for nothing. Believing in Jesus won't bring her back, but it'll give her short life more meaning than if she had lived to be a hundred."

Pa's head snapped up. The ceiling beckoned. Light from recently installed windows streamed from the rising sun, lighting the crude wooden cross in the front. The air filled with unfamiliar electric energy. Pa got up and walked to the pot-bellied stove, staring at the fire, which had taken a menacing look.

"It was all about a worn-out stove, and I'm too stubborn to get a new one."

"Friend, it's time. You must decide."

"All I do is tell him?"

"Yes, aloud."

"Was the cross painful?"

"I think so."

"Why?" The thought overwhelmed Pa.

"He loves you enough to collect your soul so you don't spend eternity in Hell." The preacher's voice was soft and tender, filled with kindness that Pa had never noticed in anyone.

"How long is eternity?"

"It never stops."

Pa took one last look at the stove's fire, took a deep breath, walked up the front, knelt at the rough-hewn cross, and blurted, "Jesus, I am so stubborn. I'm filled with stubbornness and doing wrong. I always have been. I want You to be my Barron, my Lord. I believe You died for me, and You're alive. You're God. Forgive me, please."

He looked at the preacher and broke into the broadest smile the preacher had ever seen. "I feel so different! I don't need everything to be my way. Why's it so bright in here suddenly? Thank you!"

"I suggest you surprise your family. Let them ask you about what you did. It'll be a wonderful surprise. And we'll baptize you in the spring after the weather warms up. We'll talk about that later."

Pa was already running from the church, headed to the supply store. The preacher smiled and thought, *did that guy skip? I have a sermon to work on, so I had best be about it. Sunday comes soon enough.*

4
THE BIRTH

PA WAS PANTING WHEN HE RAN UP THE SUPPLY STORE PORCH STEPS AND impatiently paced, waiting for Orney to unlock the door.

"Whoa, Mr. Schumerhass, slow down. Sorry about your little girl. Now, what brings you here so early?"

"Thank you, Orney; tell me about stoves and furnaces!" Pa's impatience was unusual.

"Well, I can get the best. What do you have in mind?"

"I'm not sure. I want something to keep my place warm."

"Well, let's look at the catalog. Here we go. This stove is the standard pot-bellied stove, which is very popular. Here's one that claims it heats better without using so much fuel. See the extra ledge on top? Your wife could set the coffee pot on it while using the stove. I think they say Franklin invented it or something like that. Does this interest you?"

Pa studied the picture. Something didn't seem right. "No, it's not what I have in mind. What else you got?"

"Well, this one's made from heavier steel. It'll last until the Master comes."

"No, I don't think so. Anything else?"

"Well, this flyer came yesterday. It's a furnace. You put it into a basement. Warm water circulates from around the firebox outside and through these pipes. We run them to radiators in every room. Look, the flyer says nothing heats like it. But it's expensive, and you'll need a separate stove for cooking. If you want top-notch, we can install this model. See, here's the firebox and places for four pots at once. It even has this little box to cook in called an oven. Look at the picture of the lady baking bread. Talk about uptown."

"Okay. Work me a price up for the furnace and the fancy stove. I have some business to occupy me for a little while, and I'll be back.

"You won't be sorry. Oh, I forgot to mention. This furnace burns both wood and coal. It's best to burn both. The flyer says using wood and coal holds the heat longer. Using coal also means you don't cut as much wood."

"Now, where will I get coal?" Pa's voice dripped with disappointment.

"As you know, we're getting a railroad here. They tell me the railroad delivers top-notch coal at a reasonable price. And, if you decide to go with the furnace, we'll tell you how to operate it. It's different. And, for sure, your missus will be impressed! You'll have the first one in town." Orney rubbed his hands together and smiled so broadly his bushy sideburns wiggled.

Pa turned and walked into the new mill next door, glancing at the latest grain prices as he entered. Several farmers leaned on the counter, hotly debating nothing but having a good time doing it. Pa addressed them, "Morning, neighbors."

Shem, who lived across town, looked at Pa. "Friend, I am so sorry about your little girl. Broke my heart." The rest nodded in agreement.

"Thank you. It broke me, not just my heart, but my will. I hurt more than I have ever hurt before.

"I am going to need quite a bit of help starting tomorrow. I'm building a basement, so it is shovel work. I'll pay a dollar per day per man, from sunup to sundown, plus noon dinner. I can use everyone that wants the work, but I want to finish the job quickly."

"Why do you want a basement?"

"I decided to put a furnace in."

"Hey, once our wives hear about this, we'll all have to do it!" The men glanced uneasily at each other.

"And we'll help each other. Spread the word, will you? Tomorrow, right after breakfast."

Pa headed back to the supply store. The farmers stared after him before Shem spoke up. "I think he lost his mind with grief. We need to help our neighbor and dig his basement. Besides, I can surely use the money."

Orney was busy making out the order. Pa never flinched even though Orney was afraid he would lose the sale. "You said I need to put this in a basement?"

"Yep. I recommend you make the walls thick concrete with a concrete ceiling. I'll make you a good deal on the concrete." Orney believed in pushing his luck.

"Why do I need concrete walls?"

"Three reasons. First, this thing won't work unless it is in a basement. If you have a fire in your coal bin, the concrete protects the rest of the house. Lastly, the concrete walls will keep the house warmer in the winter and cooler in the summer. Your potatoes won't freeze, and your fresh vegetables will last much longer. I suggest you make the basement fit under your whole house. You can make a separate room for vegetables, another for canned goods, and a third for things like creaming your milk and making butter. We can add a small room for your fuel next to your furnace room. You won't be sorry, I promise."

Pa pulled on his mustache, "Hmm, having a good place to do those things sounds like something I need.

"Okay, get the materials for a basement under the whole house. I'll make different rooms and have one for canned goods. I don't like them stacked in the dining room."

Orney decided to go for the moon. "This furnace heats water that circulates. But the water tends to evaporate. You will need a well and pump inside your house. We can install a little storage reservoir for the furnace, and your family can pump water directly into the kitchen. What say you?"

Pa never even blinked. "Okay."

"I need a down payment, then the rest on delivery. The cement takes about a week to arrive, and the rest in two weeks. I will telegraph the order this afternoon."

"Okay," Pa responded in a clipped yet cheery voice as if repeating what he knew was already decided.

"Do you have sand and gravel? You'll need them for the concrete. It's about three parts sand and three parts gravel to one part cement."

Pa growled, "I have a sandbar in the back and a gravel bar close to the road."

Orney knew how to keep a good deal and said, "Great. You could start hauling it up so it'll be ready. I suggest a seven-foot-high basement, which will have room for the pipes without them hitting your head. They'll let me know the delivery dates, and I'll tell you. I'll help install the equipment at no extra charge. Let's go and measure the house, and I'll order the right amount of cement."

The two men went back to Pa's house. Pa held one end of Orney's tape measure as he marched around, with Ma watching them through windows. Finally, Orney finished. "We'll put the pump in the kitchen and the furnace room in the center, under the parlor. The furnace has a small reservoir which you fill by opening a valve by the pump. I need to get this order worked up and on its way. Have a great day." They shook hands, and Orney walked off.

Pa whistled an unrecognizable tune as he entered the house and hung his coat up. "Morning, Ma."

"What were you and Orney doing out there? I saw you through the windows."

"Measuring the house." Pa's taciturn answer meant, "Don't ask more questions."

Dinner was stew flavored with ash and soot. The ash made liquids gritty, and the soot "poofed" into the air with every motion. The Air smelled of smoke. Everyone, especially Mae, coughed and sneezed.

"Mae, how are the chickens doing?" Pa never asked about chickens.

"They're doing very well. Most of the hens are laying plenty of eggs. The ones we're letting hatch their eggs are all sitting on them. We should have a good crop of chickens."

"Herman, what are you studying nowadays? Haven't you learned everything yet?" Pa never asked about his books.

"Ah, no, Pa. There's so much more to learn. The preacher says he'll teach me Greek if I want to know it. Not sure what to do with all this learning, though. Seems like it'd be good for something."

"Hmm. Have you ever thought about becoming a lawyer? You could go to the university in the state capital."

"Pa! I would like that very much. I have daydreamed about being a state representative, and the first step is law."

"Edith, anybody sweet on you? Do you have to fight 'em off?" Pa never had an interest in her boyfriends.

"Pa, several young men seem to like me, and I like all of them, but right now, no one's special."

"Luis, I think you should start working some land yourself. I heard there might be 40 acres for sale next to ours. Are you interested? Maybe we could trade labor or make another deal." Pa always had made it clear that Luis had to work Pa's land.

To each of the three littlest ones, Pa asked about their day or life. Usually, he couldn't relate to his youngest, but he did exceptionally well today. Ma could only stare and had trouble keeping her mouth shut.

"Ma, are you getting together with the church women this afternoon? What project do you have in mind? Where are you meeting?" Ma could hardly answer.

"Yes. We have only a little more to do on our quilt, and then we'll have made a new comforter for everyone. They look nice and will be very warm. Ida will have us over. She likes it when it's her turn."

"Be sure to take your turn and have them over. Oh yes, I need you, Edith, and Mae to plan on cooking lots of food tomorrow. I'll have many men working for me, and they'll need dinner. Well, we have work to do. Let's go, men." Pa never called his sons men. After the men left, a silence hovered over the table. The women hardly dared breathe, much less move.

"Ma, what happened to Pa?" Edith finally put into words what the women were thinking.

"I don't know. Let's keep an eye on him and make sure he's okay. He has been acting differently since morning."

During the winter, animal care and building repairs were the only farm work. Today, however, Pa, Luis, and Herman made a dragline. It wasn't much, a metal and wood box with the top and one side open. They fixed an old chain to the open side and an additional chain to the bottom. Then, they rigged it so a draft horse could pull it using hay equipment.

"Now, let's test it out back."

They went behind the barn with the draft horses. The contraption quickly removed snow from the ground. Next, they tried unsuccessfully to dig a trench in the frozen soil. Pa continued adjusting chains to no avail. Finally, he stood up and looked at Herman.

"You have any ideas? Are we going to have to break the ground with a pick?" Pa never asked for advice from his sons.

"Well, if we put a lever here, one of us could bear down on it, and the front will dig in better."

"Okay, let's try it."

The revision worked well; with practice, they could adjust how much soil each pass collected. The lever helped to dump the dirt.

"Luis, you think this is easier than by hand?"

Luis squinted at his Pa. "Yes, it is, but only if you plan on moving a lot of dirt. What're you planning, Pa?"

"Tomorrow, bright and early, we'll start building a basement under the house."

"If we rig a pully on the opposite side, the horses can pull it back into place." Herman always thought of ways to make the work easier. Secretly, while pleased, Pa worried about Herman getting a big head.

"Great idea, Herman. We can do this. I plan to dig a trench to open it up, then, using the dragline, pull the dirt out. It shouldn't be frozen under the house, making the job easier.

"I hope we get a good turnout of men from town. Now, we need some cribbing to hold the house while we work. Don't need the house falling on anyone." His plan was coming together.

The three men took the draft horses to the woodlot and felled a small oak tree. The horses effortlessly pulled the tree to the house, where the men rolled it onto blocks to raise it several inches off the ground. Pa then stood on the log and squared opposite sides using his broad ax while Herman and Luis trimmed the branches and cut the tree into 18-inch lengths, making fast progress with one on each end of the cross-cut saw. For some reason, the three men worked unusually well on this cold afternoon, laughing and joking as they made the cribbing. Under their woolen blankets, the horses stood patiently nearby, waiting for their next task, swishing their tails, their breath making tiny clouds in the cold air. Herman and Luis finished cutting the cribbing while Pa put the horses away, and then the three men picked up the scrap wood for the woodpile.

"I never noticed how pleasant freshly cut oak smells," Pa remarked. Both sons paused, thinking their father had never appreciated the pleasant things.

Ma watched them through the window while doing her work, thinking, *What's my stubborn man up to?*

Pa was up long before the next day's daylight and soon finished his chores. He patted the draft horses and whispered, "Eat your full, big guys. Today is important, and you two will need all your strength."

He headed back to the house, where Ma had breakfast ready. The stove was particularly cranky, with smoke streaming from the broken lid. Soot caked Ma's face, and her hair seemed unusually filthy. Pa said nothing, only biting his lower lip and staring at his plate. Everyone ate in silence until, after they finished, Pa, Herman, and Luis grabbed their coats and headed out.

Using a pick, Pa began breaking the frozen soil leading to the root cellar. He had only worked a short time when the first of his neighbors walked up, carrying his pick and shovel.

"Hi, neighbor. What do you need me to do?"

"Our first job is to dig a ramp down. All we need to do is make a hole into the root cellar, and then we can use the horses to pull dirt from under the house. We'll move the dirt to that side of the hill. I had the kids move everything from the cellar to inside the house yesterday. My older boys are hooking up the horses to Herman's invention, which will help. The younger ones will stack the cribbing nearby, so it'll be handy. You think I've enough cribbing?"

"Don't know. I've never done this before. If not, we can always make more."

The town's men showed up individually, except Orney, who didn't make it to the party. Even the preacher showed up, and while he usually didn't do hard work, he did pitch in. Secretly, everyone wished he would leave and get out of their way.

They first removed the door and jam leading to the root cellar. The wooden steps down were mostly rotten and easily removed. The root cellar walls were thick oak planks.

Pa looked at the planks and whistled, "I didn't realize how rotten these planks were. I would need to replace them soon. Oh, well, we don't need them now. These planks are so bad that I don't think they are good for the stove."

The men quickly stacked the rotten wood in an out-of-the-way area. The disturbed wood put a fresh, earthy smell in the air.

The workers started a dirt bucket brigade to make a trench under the house while Herman and Luis let the dragline down the hole for the ramp. Men stepped aside as the horses walked forward, filling the bucket. Luis guided the bucket using his youthful enthusiasm and, in a short time, finished the ramp and began working under the house. The men looked at the gadget with a new measure of respect.

"Neighbor, you have some invention here. After we finish, I want to dig a drainage ditch past my back twenty. You think you could help me out?"

"We can, but let's all pitch in, and the job won't take long." Pa's reputation was anything but neighborly, and the surprised men glanced at each other at his comment.

One by one, each farmer mentioned a project each one needed. Before long, everyone had a job for Herman's invention. Something made them more enthusiastic, and the work progressed faster.

Little by little, the men dug the basement, occasionally stopping to let the horses rest. In the cloudless blue sky, the sun reflected brightly on the snow. It was dark under the house but blindingly bright outside. Occasionally, each man would stagger to the well for a needed drink of water. Their eyes had adjusted by the time they went back under the house, where they became essentially blind in the darkness. Eventually, Pa hung several oil lanterns so the men could see what they were doing.

The men used their wheelbarrows to move the dirt before the dragline. Sweat poured from everyone's forehead, and outer coats soon found a pile near the front door. Each farmer started competing, trying to outwork the rest. Then, the good-natured teasing started, encouraging even harder work.

"Is that all you can put in your wheelbarrow?"

"Hey, you're stealing my dirt. Go find your own dirt." And so on.

But no one out-worked Pa, nor was anyone cheerier or more encouraging. The men knew what to do and worked with increasing enthusiasm, cribbing the house beams as they dug. The makeshift pilings, made by stacking the fresh-cut cribbing, provided temporary support to the house. Between the wheelbarrows and dragline, their progress surprised everyone.

Edith finally approached Pa, "Pa, Ma says dinner's ready."

The men carefully stacked their tools and headed into the house, where each worker washed using water from the well bucket. Per their custom, the younger men stood respectively in the dining room since there wasn't enough room for everyone to sit. The preacher cleared his throat, "Lord, thank you for this food and everyone here. Bless our families and our work. Amen."

"Edith, get the good dishes." Ma worried about who should get the best china before giving it to Pa and the other seated men. She and the girls would wait, making sure the men had enough. She didn't need to be concerned since there was more than enough. The women washed the china as each man finished so the next shift could eat.

Ma generously dished out the stew and rock-hard biscuits, which became tasty when soaked in stew. Hunger improves every meal, and fellowship turns it into gourmet dining. Everyone finished with a generous portion of Ma's pies. The strong coffee was like the sturdy men liked. In short, it was a typical noon meal for hard-working farmers. The men grew noisy as they ate, feeling the contentment of a hearty meal and good fellowship after hard work.

Pa raised his hands and cleared his throat after everyone finished, "Ma, fancy food, dishes, and service turn our little home into top-notch dining, better than any in the big city. Thank you and the other women for your hard work." Ma's face turned bright red from the unaccustomed praise and then even redder as all the men applauded.

Luis and Herman fed the livestock while the men went back to work. It seemed the afternoon went even faster until it was dark and time to stop. The farmers returned home, and Pa and his boys went inside.

"Pa, what're you people doing out there?" Ma needed to know.

"You'll see," was all Pa said.

The next day was more similar, with the men arriving early and eagerly starting, with two important exceptions. All the village women trailed their husbands, their hands full of cooking utensils and food. The women would have their party while the men had theirs and party they did. They planned to cook enough food for an army twice the size of the men outside while talking about everything under the sun.

The second exception is that Orney arrived with a brand-new stove. With several men's help, he installed the stove in a corner on a back porch and fitted a metal pipe chimney before showing Ma how to use it.

"Later on, you might want to enclose this porch but make plenty of windows. That way, the heat can leave during the summer but stay in the house during the winter."

It took Orney all morning to show Ma her new stove, all the while acting like it was his idea, but Ma knew better, and as soon as Orney left, she collapsed in a chair and cried. All the women huddled around the new stove, each telling another how they wished they could talk their spouses into getting them one and how lucky Ma was. As a result, dinner was not ready when the men came in.

"Ma, about dinner," Pa's curious tone was not demanding or angry like usual.

"I'm sorry. We were distracted. It'll be a few minutes more."

The men all started joking and laughing until they realized they needed to buy new stoves for their wives. Soon, dinner was ready, and everyone could eat. The cooks added extra meat and plenty of potatoes to the stew. Per their custom, the men ate first, then the women and children ate the leftovers. This custom ensured the men had enough fuel for their heavy work, and secretly, each wife was proud of their husband and glad to make the sacrifice. However, there was more than enough for everyone.

It took the rest of the week to finish digging the basement.

The men worked every day except Sunday when everyone went to church. Mabel, the town gossip, loudly questioned why Pa acted so differently. Ma was as puzzled as everyone. All agreed, however, that they preferred the new Pa to the old Pa.

First light on Monday, Orney walked up to Pa. "I have your cement and some steel rods for strength; you want to make the walls strong, don't you? And the brick, pipe, and pump for the well, pilings, and chimney extension. I'll bring it over in the morning."

Late Monday, Pa assembled his neighbors after they finished digging. "Men, thanks for your help. I couldn't have done it without you. The floor is level, and everything looks perfect. Now I need to put in concrete walls and install a well. Will anyone wanting a couple more days' work show up in the morning? Meanwhile, I'll settle for what we have done. I have the best neighbors in the world!"

The following day, several more farmers brought their wagons and teams. While a couple of workers set up an old feed trough to mix the concrete near their ramp, others brought up sand and gravel. Herman took Pa's horses and wagon to the back shed for lumber. Orney soon drove up with his wagon loaded with bagged cement and steel rods.

"Help me unload this. There are several more loads. I also have the brick you need for the well and columns."

They made the concrete using buckets of water from the windmill, cement, sand, and gravel. They began the back-breaking work of pouring the ceilings, using several boards as the frame. They propped the makeshift forms with additional boards before stuffing the ceiling with concrete, which splattered on the men. Their wives later complained about how hard it was to wash the concrete from their clothes. Years later, everyone could tell how much everyone did by the spots on their clothes.

Using lumber as forms, they laid courses around the basement perimeter, placed the rebar, and poured the concrete. The joking and laughing made moving concrete easier. Several farmers framed the doors to each basement room. They initially concentrated on the new furnace room to allow the concrete to cure while they finished the other rooms. The men worked together, completing one part while starting the next. Soon, it was dinner time. This time, because they were pouring concrete, the men ate in shifts while the others continued working.

"Ma was beside herself. All the women in town came to try out the new stove and cooked more food than anyone could remember. Each one worked on it, not even leaving room for Ma to stir the soup.

Shem and his brothers were the village well diggers. They installed the new inside water well in the basement under where the sink would go, lining it with bricks. "You won't run out of water in that well. It flows better than most we've built. That is surprising since you are on this hill. It must be trying to make a spring near here."

"Thanks again for your help," Pa said, very gratefully.

Now, the men finished for the day and promised to be back in the morning.

First thing in the morning, the preacher's wife came over and spoke to Ma. "You need to come with me. I want your help at my place. The other women said they would take care of the cooking. In fact, why don't you and the girls spend a few nights and get away from this hectic mess."

"I'm not sure. There is so much to do here."

"Ha! They'll take care of it. You need a break. Come on; I'll help you get your things. You're always working, and it'll be good for you."

Without taking "no" for an answer, she herded Ma and both girls out the door and down the road.

By now, the concrete had cured enough to remove the forms, making it easier for the rest of the basement pour.

Orney showed up a few minutes later and installed the new sink and pump while the men poured concrete. They routed the sink drain into the new basement and through the wall such that it spilled on the ground several feet from the house. They covered the drain pipe with several feet of dirt and put gravel under the discharge. The hill made the drain work easier. This drain arrangement would keep the water from freezing until it was well past the house. The hand pump first filled a sink reservoir. Simple valves routed water to either the sink or the furnace's reservoir.

Orney showed them where to make holes through the floor for the pipes, and the different men eagerly began drilling. It was hard work going through the heavy oak flooring and fresh concrete. The workers quickly ate a simple meal and eagerly returned to work since everyone itched to see the new-fangled contraption in operation.

Now, Orney showed them how to connect radiators. They put two in the dining room, two in the parlor, and one in each bedroom, all under windows. Night came, and everyone went home. Pa remarked to Luis, "The house is quiet without Ma and your sisters."

The next day, the men returned and finished pouring concrete. The furnace room was under the parlor, which meant removing the parlor stove and extending the brick chimney into the basement for the new furnace. They poured the basement floor, moving the temporary cribbing as needed before replacing the cribbing with sturdy brick columns.

They quickly finished the rest of the basement, laying plank over the curing concrete for the workers to walk on. Orney brought the furnace and installed it, along with the water reservoir and the second pump. The new brick columns securely held the house while the local carpenter used his level to confirm it sat perfectly. Someone threw the cribbing into the new coal bin.

Finally, they finished the basement. They installed a small steel door in the concrete wall leading to the little coal bin next to the furnace room, backfilled and leveled dirt in the ramp and along the basement walls. Pa could unload coal and wood directly into the coal bin through the steel door. Orney invented the name, and it stuck, even though they wouldn't have coal for a few weeks. Pa only stood and stared at it. He could back his wagon to it and unload fuel without carrying a stick from the woodpile. In his mind, an inside wood pile became the new pinnacle of luxury. They installed inside and outside doors and built steps on the opposite side of the furnace room. He could reach his new furnace from either outside or inside the house. The house looked the same as it always had after the farmers had finished. No one could suspect it now had a basement.

Orney couldn't resist giving advice, "You best carry the ashes up these steps and not take them through the house. You'll be surprised how pleased it'll make your missus. I'll get coal when the railroad's finished in a few months. Until then, only burn hardwood, and make sure it burns hot. Even better, if the wood is several months old and dry, that'll keep the tar from building up in your chimney and causing a fire. I don't know much about them, only what the flyer warns."

Pa only nodded, wondering what he had gotten into.

The next day, the entire town, except for the preacher's wife, Ma, Edith, and Mae, gathered at Pa's place. They loaded a wagon with cut oak, backed the team to the steel door, and quickly unloaded it.

"Now, men, we must let this wood thaw a little. While we do that, let's take the old stoves out and clean up." Orney liked being in charge, mostly pretending to know what he was doing. Pa didn't understand what he meant by "thawing the wood" but decided it didn't matter. Orney sometimes said things that made little sense.

He showed Pa, and as many that could fit in the furnace room, how to fill the reservoir, how to start a fire, how fast it burned, and warned him again about burning green wood. The furnace woke when the tinder lit, momentarily confused by all the farmers crowding around it.

The furnace felt like a child, burping water from the water jacket into the pipes. It became aware of each room, sensing people, furniture, clothing, and the emotions of everyone present. It somehow knew where the old pot-belled stoves had been but now were missing. A sensitivity for those stoves it replaced tempered its youthful enthusiasm. *Well,* it thought, *out with the old and in with the new. It is the way of life. I hope this guy takes care of me. I have a big job and will need a lot of fuel.*

Orney continued, "Sappy wood causes chimney fires. You might burn your house down. Use dry, hardwood, like oak, until they bring the coal I ordered. If you only have fresh-cut wood, be sure to make the fire hot. That will burn the sap before it gets to the chimney. Do you see the water temperature gauge reading in the green band? We're ready to make sure the water circulates properly."

They went upstairs, and Orney ceremoniously opened a radiator bleed valve, holding a small can under the spout. Hot steam whistled out, and soon, water sputtered through the valve. Orney closed the valve and moved to the next radiator. The furnace felt more vigorous and alive as each radiator experienced the excitement of the flowing hot water.

"Check the reservoir after you blow the air from each radiator to ensure we have enough water. Right now, we're filling pipes and need more water than normal. You should bleed air, I think, every week or so. The piping's crooks and crannies trap air, making it less efficient. It will work better after a few weeks. Now your house will be nice and warm, better than the Barron's castle ever was."

They went from radiator to radiator, bleeding air and checking the reservoir and water temperature. Each man excitedly shouted conflicting advice, like children at Christmas. Everyone kept looking into the firebox, ostensibly making sure it was hot enough, but, in reality, they were enamored with the furnace. The furnace enjoyed the attention and was amazed at how thirsty it was.

"Orney, explain again how the hot water gets from the furnace to the second floor. It is a long distance." Pa wondered.

Orney smiled, "It is one of the wonders of modern technology. The water jacket is around the firebox. You have seen steam from a tea kettle rise, haven't you?" Pa nodded. "The hot water makes its way to the radiators, where the heat leaves the water and warms the room. The cooler water wants to go down, so it enters the down pipes for a return visit to the water jacket. We must remove the air so the water can reach the radiators. Once the circulation starts, it goes faster and increases the efficiency. We left the floor vents to help the second story stay warm. You are correct that it is a long way, making it harder for the hot water to get there. Regardless, I am confident it works. The city municipal offices have these, and they work fine. I am sure there is more to it, but this is all I know. The city janitor told me how much the office workers complained when he didn't bleed the air, so I know it is crucial.

"Oh yes, I almost forgot. These valves in the radiator inlets can control the hot water flow each radiator gets. This way, you can control each room if it gets too hot or you don't use it."

At long last, it was time to show Ma their new extravagance. The furnace was burning wood, Orney had bled the air from all the radiators, and the house was comfortable. Pa urgently exclaimed to Herman, "Go get your mother! Hurry!"

When she entered the house, Ma demanded, "Okay, now what's all this fuss about? What's going on around here, what with all the secrecy? I think it's about time for me to know what you people are doing to my house..."

Her voice trailed off as she first saw her beat-up pot-bellied stoves were gone, then the new radiators. She collapsed into a chair and weakly asked, "What's this? Where are the stoves? What are those things under the windows?"

"It's a whole-house furnace. I decided we needed it. It's the most modern there is. Do you like it?" Pa became a little boy again, needing her approval. All she could do was cry, then jump up and hug him, burying her joyful tears into his shirt. Now, it was his turn to have a bright red face. He helplessly raised both hands, not knowing what to do with them. Everyone cheered as they filed out and went home, each wife asking her husband when they would get theirs.

⟨∾୭⟩

Pa smiled at the furnace. "And that's how you were born, my friend. It wasn't long ago, but now you're a part of our family. We had quite the learning to do. Sometimes, I fed you too much, forcing us to open the outside doors because the house became so hot. Once, right after we installed you, I forgot to feed you before I went to bed. Before morning, the kitchen water froze. We had to melt ice and boil water on the stove to thaw our pump. Heh, heh, heh, Ma was scary mad that time. Oh well, live and learn.

"Ma found out that clothes dried better when draped over the radiators. She liked it more than having them freeze on the clothesline. She still washes them in the washtub, but you even made laundry much easier.

"I wish we could do something about needing a bath weekly.

"Best of all, we discovered we could put buckets of water on the radiators, and you magically heated them. Our baths and Ma's laundry are much more enjoyable with warm water. And everyone gets their clean water. Maybe baths aren't so bad after all."

The furnace, proud to improve its family's lives, burned the fuel brightly. Pa checked the firebox, ash bin, and water temperature before adjusting the airflow and lumbering upstairs, yawning and stretching as he went.

⟨∾୭⟩

5
THE WEDDING

PA ENTERED THE FURNACE ROOM AND CHECKED THE FIRE. IT WAS OKAY, just like it had been the previous time and the time before that.

"Well, Mr. Furnace, I guess I'm nervous. You're the only sane one around here. Everyone else is rushing around like ants, especially the women. They keep sending me down here, most likely to get me out of their way."

The furnace's brightly burning fire added cheeriness to the tiny room. Mr. Furnace was determined to do his part on this special day.

"I don't know why they want to be married here, in our parlor, instead of in the church. It's not that cold outside, and spring is nearly here. But you only marry once, so whatever they want is fine with me. I guess it's tradition, like having funerals in the parlor. The church makes more sense. We mustn't go against traditions, can we, Mr. Furnace?"

Most of the guests stood in the parlor, which had more room now that the old pot-bellied stove was gone. The ambitious young groom, who already owned 120 acres, stood facing West. The preacher stood with his back to the bay windows, secretly glad for the warm radiator behind him. Edith glided in on Pa's arm and faced East, looking splendid in her new, store-bought dress.

The preacher cleared his throat and began.

"In the Name of The Father, The Son, and The Holy Ghost. We gathered to witness this fine couple join in marriage. Just as the Bride of Christ looks to the East for the Second Coming, Edith looks East for her beloved."

Pa wasn't sure about the Bride of Christ looking one way or the other, maybe up, but the preacher loved these stories. The preacher then droned on about the creation story, telling of God creating Adam. Still, Adam needed a woman, so God made Eve. He pontificated on other marriages, Sarah and Abraham, more brave women and grateful husbands. He expounded on Proverbs 31, discussing the ideal wife, and passages where Paul exhorts husbands to love their spouses. Everyone had heard the same message at every wedding, and most could repeat it word for word. Yet, they all nodded and gave him their total attention as if hearing it for the first time. The furnace listened carefully through the radiators, pleased with the sentiments.

The couple pronounced their vows with conviction. As they did, Pa felt a little sick in his stomach as he realized Edith was no longer his. No one noticed his tiny tear.

Eventually, the preacher said, "I pronounce you man and wife."

Pa thought it was Herman who whispered, "Finally."

Mr. Furnace was proud. He kept the room warm, and while the outside was not freezing, it was still chilly.

The women served a meal, and suddenly, everyone was gone. They shook the groom's hand and carefully kissed the bride on their way out. Most put a little money in a basket by the door to help the new couple start their new life. The lovebirds walked to the groom's house, eager to begin married life.

Ma and Mae cleaned up. "Didn't Edith just glow? She looked so happy!"

"Yes, Ma. It makes me want to think about my wedding soon."

"Don't make it too soon," growled Pa.

Later, Ma found Pa sitting in the furnace room, talking to the furnace. "Well, Mr. Furnace, Edith moved out. She found herself an excellent young man she would be proud of. They'll live nearby but don't have nearly as good a furnace as ours. Someday, they will.

"My parents all died before we left the old country, as did Ma's. It was only our little family, and I felt such a responsibility. Leaving was the best decision I've ever made, except for deciding to serve Jesus. Soon, Herman will go to the university, and Mae will marry also. Luis will most likely want to take over the farm. He'll do well. He's a hard worker, built like a bull, and farm-smart. I'm not sure about the three younger boys. They're too young to know how they'll turn out."

"Pa, you okay?" Ma hesitated before entering the furnace room.

"Yeah, I'm okay, Ma. I'm feeling a little down about Edith moving out."

"But Pa, our job is to raise them, not live their lives for them. We did a fine job, and you did, too. Now it's their turn to live their own lives. Soon, they'll have children for us to enjoy."

"Thanks, Ma. I'm very happy for Edith but also a little sad. Aren't you sad she's gone?"

"I miss the little girl struggling to cut wood and always trying to help. But, well, we must move on. Come on, stop talking to the furnace, and come upstairs. It's getting late." She tenderly put her hand on his shoulder and quietly mused, *for years, I could never show him any affection. He was like a faraway, rocky island.* Pa gently laid his hand on Ma's and looked at her, his eyes glistening in the reflection from the furnace.

"I'll be up in a minute. I want to make sure the fire will last the night."

It's not that cold outside, muttered Ma. *He needs to be alone with his thoughts. He's definitely a different man, but he still has a stubborn streak.*

"Mr. Furnace, you look like you have a good burn. Let me put another log on and check the ash level." Pa turned his attention to the furnace, checking the ash bin, the water level in the reservoir, and the water temperature before studying the fire.

The furnace burned a little brighter, telling Pa it liked him spending time talking to it. It knew summer sleep was coming soon.

Pa saw something in the fire, maybe only a flicker of light, and began weeping. His cries started softly but soon rose in volume until they echoed throughout the house. "My baby. My stubbornness sent her into the fires of Hell. Why does Jesus love a person like me?"

Ma rushed down to the furnace room. "Pa, what's wrong?"

"Ma, I'm so sorry about the baby. I was so wrong, so stubborn, so selfish. How can you forgive me? How can you love me? How can anyone?"

"Pa, you did the best you could. You don't know what happened to her. The Preacher is right, 'God loves her and will take care of her, even in death. She was too little to make her own decisions.' And you did something, giving us this wonderful furnace, the new stove, and even indoor water! We're the first ones in the area with things not even the Barron had. Pa, I forgive you, and I love you. I loved you then and still do, despite your faults."

Pa leaned his head against his wife while she stroked his hair. She noticed it was turning gray and rough. Pa could only cry until, at long last, the tears dried up. Ma wiped his eyes with her apron, put her arms around his head, and hugged him tightly.

Finally, Pa changed the airflow by adjusting the ash door. Pa hugged his wife, "Thank you so much. You're so special. I love you."

Ma again wondered about Pa's unusual tenderness, but something bonded them closer than ever. Ma gently led Pa by the hand up the stairs, where they went into the parlor and sat quietly next to each other, Ma leaning on Pa's shoulder.

That was the last fire in the furnace that winter. The warmer weather let the furnace rest for the summer, although it was aware of everything in the house. The family was busier than ever, planting crops, harvesting alfalfa, pulling weeds, tending the garden, raising chickens, cattle, and hogs, and harvesting their crops. Once again, the farm did very well, and after the harvest, the neighbor accepted Luis' bid for the 40 acres. Pa was proud that Luis bought it without his help. The two men agreed to farm together.

That year, one of the draft horses stumbled. Pa rubbed it down, especially paying attention to the game leg. Both horses were old and needed replacing. Pa knew it but struggled to admit it. He spent the night on his stool in the barn, talking with the horses, their tired souls failing to shine through their dull eyes. They had given their all. When morning came, Ma found him weeping with his head buried in the mane of the limping horse. Without saying a word, she put her hand on his shoulder and waited.

"Well, Ma, I think we need new draft horses."

"I'm sorry."

"Yep, we have had these since we got here and Oscar before us. They have served us well but are old and worn out now. Nothing left to do."

That afternoon, Pa hitched his carriage horse to their buggy. "Luis, will you come with me?" And the two were off. A larger village lay several miles down the corduroy road, where a stock dealer did business. They found him, and, as luck had it, he had four giant draft horses for sale. They were young, gentle, and well-mannered. Luis tied the animals to the back of the buggy while Pa paid for them.

"You'd think this guy was selling his children, the price he charged," Pa grumbled as they drove back to the farm. They put the new horses in the barn and turned the older ones into the pasture.

"Pa, what you going to do with the old ones?" Luis didn't want to know, but at the same time, he needed to know.

"I haven't decided."

They needn't have thought about it, for a couple of days later, the game horse stumbled, fell, and couldn't get up. They buried it in the pasture near the woods. Pa delayed making any decision about the other, which appeared lonely and depressed. One day, Pa went into town, returning with a little puppy. Pa turned the mutt loose into the pasture and watched it trot toward the behemoth. The family observed it sit in front of the old steed, looking up with pitiful, puppy eyes. The horse stretched his nose and touched the dog's nose, who began licking the giant's face. The new best friends became inseparable, with the puppy struggling to keep up with the old horse. Later, after the horse finally succumbed to old age, the puppy often went to the grave to sit for a little while before returning to the barn to spend time with the other horses.

The new horses were strong and pulled equipment with ease. *The extra horses have helped more than I realized. We don't have to rest the animals as often. We should have done this long ago.* Pa needed to reassure himself that the extra cost was worth it.

Luis became stronger than his father, who proudly watched him mature.

The summer ended, and Pa went to the furnace room early on one crisp morning. "Okay, Mr. Furnace, it's time for you to wake up and get to work."

The kindling and logs began burning, heating the water. Slowly, hot water rose through the furnace's metal veins, reaching the radiators throughout the house before returning to the reservoir. It didn't take long before the furnace was happily heating the homestead. Pa went from radiator to radiator, bleeding air.

The furnace knew everything in the house. It knew the whispered secrets of Ma and Pa, the fights between children, and Mae's continual nightmares of ghost chickens.

Herman soon left for the University, catching the train to the capital. Mae and Luis returned to the house while Ma and Pa lingered on the platform.

"Ma, another one's all grown up." Pa sadly watched him leave.

"Yes, that's the way it works. Luis is grown as well. Fine men they are; they make us proud."

They paused for a few minutes, Ma staring straight ahead, watching the tracks where the train left. Finally, she couldn't stand it any longer and exclaimed, "Edith will have a child."

Pa whirled around to look at his wife. "What did you say?"

"Edith's pregnant."

Pa almost jumped, swinging his wife high in the air around him. "Wonderful! You aren't very good at keeping secrets, are you!"

"Hey, put me down before you break something. What will people think if they see us? You ready to go home?" Ma laughed.

The crops were finally all in barns before winter came in full force. Once a month, Pa took his wagon to Orney's store and returned with a load of coal. They cut wood, laughed, hardly ever missed church, and visited with the other farmers. Pa never let anyone else feed the furnace.

Pa always made time to see how his new grandson was doing. While the furnace was happy because Pa was happy, it was sad because Pa didn't visit as long. He no longer told the old stories like before but instead made up for it by telling the furnace all about Edith's family.

Two weeks after Edith's wedding, tragedy struck the village. Mabel Fushusy's husband, Claude, was re-shingling their house after a thunderstorm damaged the shingles. Pa and the other villagers brought their spare shingles, and everyone began helping.

Claude's house was the largest in the area. Mabel always bragged about their prosperity, but everyone wondered how true it all was since

Claude's crops were usually the poorest in the neighborhood. He didn't own much land and only one draft horse.

Claude was at the roof's highest point when he slipped, tumbling off and hitting a wagon's edge. His scream startled the horse, which lurched. No one understood what happened, only that Claude was unresponsive. His funeral several days later was unremarkable.

Mabel loudly blamed everyone, but especially Claude. Her grief converted her to a bitter, angry woman whose only pleasure was reporting on other's misfortunes. She imagined problems when she ran out of actual gossip. Mabel sold the farmland and turned the house into a boarding house. Her business was close to the train station, making it convenient for railroad workers and travelers. Her cooking was far better than her disposition. Eavesdropping on her clients gave her much of the news. However, it did not take long for most villagers to nod and smile politely while conveniently forgetting most of what she said.

The following fall, the furnace woke again to banish the chill from the house.

6

THE STORM

THE FAMILY FINISHED THEIR SUNDAY DINNER ONE APRIL AND BEGAN relaxing while enjoying each other's company.

Ma looked out the window and commented, "My, but that wind is starting to rise."

Pa walked out to the porch. "That sky is starting to look green. The clouds are swirling, and the air smells different. Listen, our cattle are upset. Luis, we better move them to the barn before that storm is upon us."

The two men rushed to the pasture and began moving cattle into the barn. Several didn't want to go.

"Luis, get some rope and a couple of bags. We will have herd these frightened animals to safety."

Luis returned with bags and rope, which the two men used to lead the cattle into the barn. After closing the doors, they turned their attention to the other animals. For whatever reason, the pigs, sheep, and chickens were all safely inside, allowing them to close the doors.

"Luis, we should check on our neighbors to see if anyone needs help. Bring the ropes and bags."

The two men walked from farm to farm, looking for animals that they could help put into shelter. They finally reached the far side of town, where Nievelle Sothe lived. Nievelle was a long-term resident that had terrible luck. He had no children, and his wife had just died. His ground was on a clay ridge, which did not grow crops well. Three of his frightened cattle had broken through the fence. Pa saw Nievelle trying to herd them back to his barn with little success.

Pa put a bag over two of the animal's heads, and using their ropes, he and Luis led the animals to the shelter. Once inside, they returned and secured the last one.

"Thank you so much," Nievelle said. "It is hard for one person to herd these stubborn animals."

Pa smiled, "Look, Ma has saved pie for us. How about coming over and enjoying it with us? She would be disappointed if you don't."

"I really shouldn't," replied Nievelle. "But, I will, to be neighborly."

The men returned to Pa's house, where they sat on the porch to watch the incoming storm. Ma brought everyone pie, even though Pa and Luis already had a piece. Ma knew Nievelle never had good meals and ensured his slice was the largest.

"Look at the strange cloud," exclaimed Ma. "It seems to twist and snake from the sky toward the ground."

They watched, in fascination, as it reached the ground. It turned black as soon as it touched the ground, and they could see trees being uprooted and thrown into the air. A horrifying noise filled the air, giant hailstones began pounding the buildings, and massive lightning bolts streaked across the sky.

Luis galvanized everyone by yelling, "That is a tornado. Quick, we must get into the basement. We must leave everything and run for our lives."

As soon as they reached the basement, they crouched against a wall. The deafening noise came from directly overhead and then was gone. Pa cautiously went upstairs, checking to confirm it was safe. The tornado had lifted before reaching their house. The furnace breathed a sigh of relief. It could sense the family's fear and relief once it was over. The storm continued, pelting everything with torrential rain.

Luis walked on the porch and looked toward town. He could see smoke rising from the far side despite the rain.

"Pa, it looks like something is on fire. We should go see if we can help."

Nievelle looked at the smoke, "That is coming from near my place!"

As they soon discovered, it was Nievelle's hay barn. He had a different type of barn, which was a single-story shed. This arrangement made it easier for the farmer to store his alfalfa but made it harder to feed his animals. A massive lightning bolt had struck and ignited the barn. The fire destroyed the barn, and the alfalfa began burning. It would also be a total loss. The rain had changed to a slight drizzle.

Nievelle stared at the fire, watching it burn. There was nothing anyone could do to save any of his alfalfa. He dropped to his knees and began weeping.

"Martha, I am so sorry. No matter how hard I try, it never works out. I can't raise decent crops; now even my alfalfa is ruined. Why did you have to die? I don't know what to do."

Pa put his hand on Nievelle's shoulder. "Luis, go get a wagon load of alfalfa for our neighbor."

The rain stopped before Luis returned with feed for the animals.

Nievelle put his head into his hands and continued weeping, giant sobs shaking his body. No one knew what to say.

Suddenly, Nievelle moaned, which Pa thought was the scariest sound he had ever heard. As Nievelle gasped and clutched his chest, he fell forward. The doctor was in the crowd and immediately came to Nievelle's aid. But it was too late.

The preacher looked at Pa, "You are one of his best friends. Will you take care of things?" The crowd murmured their agreement.

Most of the village attended Nievelle's funeral. There wasn't any family to comfort, but they all felt awkward. Frontier life was hard, with frequent deaths. Usually, however, there was family to keep going. Somehow, this was so different that it bothered everyone.

Pa used his alfalfa to feed the cattle until he could sell them and the draft horse. He and Ma began going through the house, looking for relative's addresses. Finally, there was an unopened letter with the return address of what they discovered was a distant cousin who lived in Connecticut. Pa sent him a telegraph. Nievelle had a few sheep and chickens, which Pa decided to buy. He put all the money into a small can until he heard back from his cousin.

No one farmed Nievelle's land that year. It was nearly August when a stranger came to town, asking for Pa.

"Hello. I am Mathew Soethe, Nievelle's cousin. His father and mine were brothers. I had written him once but never received a reply, which is unsurprising because he didn't know how to read. I understand you are settling his estate?"

"That's right. Come, how about we visit Nievelle's house."

"I can't stay long. I have to get back to my business. I was shocked when I heard about Nievelle. He had a difficult life despite trying so hard."

They walked through the house. Mathew chose two small things.

Pa gave Mathew the money from the animal sales. "I don't need his money. All I want are these tokens from my cousin. Will you sell his property? You can keep the money."

Pa nodded, and the men returned to Pa's house, where Ma had a meal ready. Mathew left the next day.

Pa sold Nievelle's property for a fair price to a young man starting his farming business. He did better than Nievelle, eventually buying more and better ground.

Pa walked to the town clerk's office. Joe Losten, who filled this position, was working on official duties.

"Joe, is there a way to telegraph this money to Mathew Soethe? It is the sale price of Nievelle's place. Mathew is Nievelle's only heir."

"I can take care of it," Joe answered and gave Pa a receipt.

Later, the preacher walked by the clerk's office.

"Hey, preacher. I can't believe what Pa Schumerhass just did. He is sending all of Nievelle's money to Nievelle's heir. Pa could have kept some back for his trouble, and no one would have known."

The preacher smiled, remembering the kind of person Pa used to be. "Yes, he is an incredibly honest man. We should thank the Lord we have him for a neighbor."

Pa would have been embarrassed if he had known this story would circulate. But, like in most small towns, there are no secrets.

7
THE BANK

ONE OF THE FIRST THINGS OSCAR HAD TAUGHT PA HAD TO DO WITH money. The little village had a small bank, if you could call it that, which was no more than a large iron safe in the town clerk's office. The clerk kept a ledger with one page for each customer, which listed deposits, withdrawals, and a running total. The clerk was one of the friendliest citizens, well-respected, and very careful. He charged a small fee to keep people's money safe and rarely made loans.

More complicated banking was in the larger city. They made loans and paid interest on any deposits. Once, Pa asked Oscar why he didn't trust the larger bank.

"I don't know. The bankers wear fancy clothes, their hands are soft, and some have that thin mustache. I never trust anyone who can't decide whether they want a beard. I don't know them like I know our banker. He has always been fair to me, and that is good enough for my business."

The clerk's safe saved the farmers from making trips to the city. Most of their transactions were small and between themselves, except when they paid their taxes. Every farmer kept a few dollars in an old jar, which they used when they paid each other for helping with alfalfa or other farm work. It didn't take long for the paper money to become worn as they passed the same bill back and forth.

The clerk's position was an elected one. He treated everyone fairly, although sometimes he was a pompous bureaucrat. He loved bringing news of a farmer inheriting property and other official business. The town had voted a small property tax, which he also collected. The villagers paid their other taxes in the larger city. Most people gave the banker their excess, only making a yearly trip to the city to pay taxes, deposit their accumulated funds, or withdraw savings for major purchases. Every person was proud of their word and couldn't think of breaking it. The supply store business was cash only, as was the boarding house. Mabel paid with paper money for her eggs, chickens, and other supplies. Typically, her borders were the community's only source of "fresh" bills.

Pa was even more conservative. His prosperous vegetable business and crop and cattle sales made Pa the village's most successful farmer. Pa made regular deposits into the bank after each trip to the city but kept most of his earnings in a crock by his bed. It didn't take long before it overflowed.

What should I do with this money? I hate opening an account at the city bank. Our local guy can only accept so much. I hope no one decides to rob him. All they would have to do is drag his safe to a hideout where they could work on opening it at their leisure. I'm not too fond of having that much money around the house. It is good that no one else knows about it, but you never know what will happen. Burying it raises more problems. Pa considered, nay worried, about his situation as he worked.

One day, at the noon meal, Ma asked Pa, "You are acting preoccupied lately. What is going on? Is there something wrong?"

"Ma, I have a farm problem I am working on. Our farm has done very well, and I am deciding what to do next. Should I buy more land, another team of horses, or what?"

Ma paused, then answered, "The Bible says that we should be content with what we have and trust that God will take care of us. He always has, and I see no reason He won't in the future."

Pa became gruff, "I know. Yet, He expects us to be responsible with what He gave us. I need to do noon chores."

Pa worried more about his money. It wasn't that he wanted more or was afraid a thief would steal it; he did not know what to do. Ma noticed that he spent more time with the furnace but sat staring at it instead of telling it his problems. It was even more strange because it was too hot to build a fire.

Pa's worrying went on for several weeks until, one day, a neighbor ran up. "Where is Pa? We all need to meet at the church. They are saying something terrible thing has happened."

Luis ran to the cornfield, where Pa was hoeing weeds. "Pa, we need to meet at the church. Some emergency has happened. I don't know anything else."

Pa ran to the shed and put his hoe away. Then, the family rushed to the packed church. Nearly everyone in the village was present, and most were talking excitedly. Pa couldn't make out what had happened in all the excitement.

The preacher stood up and motioned for quiet. "Neighbors, we must remain calm. We all know our banker is a decent person. I am sure it will work out. Let me open in prayer."

After the prayer, Joe stood and motioned for quiet. "Neighbors, thank you for letting me act as your local banker. I'll begin by saying that everyone's money is safe and available as you might need it. Nothing is changing in that regard."

The crowd noticeably relaxed. Rumors had flown about how the money had been stolen or lost or the records had messed up. The people were still shifting uncomfortably in their seats but now were willing to listen.

Joe continued. "You probably know a bank examiner came by my office earlier this week. I'm unsure what he was looking for, but he reviewed all the books, counted the cash, looked at the safe, and gave me the once-over. It was uncomfortable. He kept asking how I didn't know if money was missing and tried to accuse me of theft. The last thing he said was that everything was in order and that he would send me a letter stating that. I will post his letter in my office so anyone can read it.

"That was the good news. The man did say that our little bank needed to make changes. That means applying for a charter, forming a corporation, and possibly upgrading the building. Some laws will change how we do business, and I will be the first to admit I don't know what they are. He promised to mail me more information.

"The next step is to decide if we want a local bank. We don't need one if we are willing to use the one in the city. I can give everyone their money back, and you can make your deposits. We will set up the corporation and elect directors if we want a local bank.

"Having a local bank means we can lend ourselves money for emergencies. We loaned Matt Gretta several hundred dollars to purchase new draft horses after wolves killed his. He paid us back after harvest time."

Some citizens were upset Joe used their money for loans. They knew Matt and trusted him. They didn't like not knowing what was happening with their hard-earned money.

Joe continued, "If we do this, the new bank will pay an interest rate on deposits and charge a higher interest rate on loans. Money that is not loaned will be deposited in the city bank, earning interest. Everyone is permitted to buy stock in the bank company, and stockholders will receive profits as a dividend.

"The bank will use the money from the stock sale to meet the new regulations. Any leftover will be deposited and earn interest, boosting the dividends.

"I don't understand why the examiner looked at our books unless we have enough deposits to become a real bank. He is probably concerned that we might be robbed and everyone is out. Regardless, we set ourselves up as a bank, or you must move your funds to the city bank. I'm sorry about this."

The chatter in the room rose as the farmers tried to make sense of what the banker had said. Many of the men did not trust bankers, or any authority for that matter. They all had terrible experiences at one time or another, and this news did not sit well.

Orney walked to the front and raised his hand for quiet. "You said that we must form a corporation if we do this. What is that exactly, and how do we do it?"

Joe smiled. "A corporation is owned by people, in this case, you folks. We will sell stock to whoever wants some. That money becomes our capital. We can use it to buy a better safe, make loans, or deposit funds in the city bank. The bank returns profits to the stockholders as deposits. Stockholders elect men to the board of directors, who then choose a president. The board hires staff and recommends any improvements. It is essential to select responsible board members.

"Corporations must have an annual meeting to explain the business to the shareholders.

"We will develop a charter, which tells the bank how to operate. The stockholders will keep some decisions for a general vote. The charter has several parts. One part is on file with the state, and the other is maintained locally. I don't have much more information, but I know some laws apply. The examiner implied that he could enforce those rules now if he wanted to. I don't know if that is true or only a threat. If we do this, we must find a lawyer to help us and file the paperwork."

Dealing with a lawyer made many even more uncomfortable.

"Does everyone have to buy stock?" Asked a young man.

"No, only those that want to," Joe answered.

"Will you have to have stock to use this new bank?"

Joe smiled, "I don't have stock in the city bank, and most of you don't either. Yet, we all use it. We would be no different."

"How much stock do we need?"

"I don't know yet. We need more information about capital requirements, etc." Joe tried to be optimistic despite his sinking feeling.

More questions followed, many of which Joe had previously answered. Joe always did his best to respond, but the sweat on his forehead belied his nervousness.

Eventually, everyone returned to their farm chores, except a few farmers clustered in the supply store to worry. As one participant left, another took their place. Orney noticed that only emotion was displayed, with no new facts. Finally, suppertime came, and the store emptied. Orney had only listened, knowing it was bad business to interject his thoughts.

Mabel was quick to question the banker's honesty. She asked anyone who would listen if he was selling the stock to line his pockets or what he intended to do with their deposits. Ironically, Mabel was a significant depositor in the existing bank and bought more bank stock than most villagers. Years later, after she died, people realized how wealthy she was. Her money didn't bring her pleasure when she lived and certainly didn't after she died. Everything went to a distant relative who sold the boarding house and the stock, only to disappear from the village forever. Mabel did demonstrate that proverb that bitter people live the longest.

That evening, Ma and Pa sat on their porch. Other neighbors made it a point to walk over and express equally uninformed opinions. Pa listened, usually without comment. He had not decided what to do but was open to all options. Finally, as the sun began hiding behind the horizon and everyone went home, Pa went to the furnace room.

"Mr. Furnace, I know you are asleep, but I must talk with you. I have a fair amount of money. Joe is a good man, but I don't know what to do.

"Lord, what do you want me to do?" Pa prayed his simple prayer over and over until finally, he rose and went to bed.

"Ma, what do you think?"

"God has always taken care of us. We should do the best we know how and trust Him. I know there is always inner peace when we do what He wants. Sometimes, He tells us plainly; at other times, it is obvious, yet most decisions are hard. If we can get our fears and desires out of the way, He will guide us. Besides, He has promised to care for us if we make mistakes. Don't think you have enough power to mess His plans up."

"Do you want to be a preacher? You are starting to sound like one."

Ma laughed, "No, our preacher can have his job. Let's go to sleep."

At breakfast the next day, Pa announced, "I have decided to buy stock in this bank. It will help support our little village and make things easier for everyone. Now I have to decide how much I should buy. We have had several good years, giving us plenty."

Later, Pa found the banker busy with his clerical duties. "Let me bother you for a moment, Joe. I want to invest in this bank. How many have decided to join me?"

Joe smiled and said, "About half the village signed up. Everyone will have to buy less stock if we have more participants. Still, it is a fair bit of money. Would you help get it started? Orney, our preacher, and Mr. Heiselmeyer have also agreed. You four are enough to get started as an interim board. We will have a stockholder's meeting after we get our charter to elect board members."

"I am not sure. I am a simple farmer and don't know much about business."

"That is not true. You have a very successful farm. You do as well as you are doing by using good business sense. The difference between the good and the best is whether someone lets their pride get in their way. When necessary, you learn and try to make the best decisions. You admit when you make a mistake and move forward, like when you planted corn too late to mature. You can learn about banking, at least enough to be a board member."

"Let me think about it, and I will let you know in a few days."

Pa talked about it to the furnace for a while that night. Like always, he spoke to God using the furnace as a surrogate, trying to sense His will. "Mr. Furnace, I think God wants me to do this. I don't want to. I am happy raising my family and animals here on my little farm. Being a banker board member is too fancy for me. It is something that others may aspire to, but mostly to show off how important they are. I'm going to bed."

It was raining the following day. Soft and steady, the rain was a farmer's dream, allowing the ground to drink the life-giving moisture. Every plant slurped as much water as possible while the ground soaked the rest of the rain, replenishing moisture through the root zone. Soon, the shallow streams and creeks would sing the melodic sounds of excess water reaching the river.

The rain turned the Cordory Road's rotting timber into a muddy slush of splinter and dirt. The ditch the villagers dug beside the road filled and began moving water. Like on every street where horses were the main form of transportation, the rain also washed the horse droppings. People generally walked around the mounds, except the rain made the roads a mess. In other words, you couldn't tell what you were stepping into.

After breakfast, Pa stood on the porch and watched the raindrops dance as they splashed into the puddles. Ma soon joined him, quietly standing beside her husband while marveling how God provided for their livelihood. The gentle rain brought the pleasant smell of promise.

Pa finally spoke, "It looks like today will be a rest day for us. We won't be able to do much besides feeding the animals."

Ma nodded before answering, "What will you tell Joe?"

Pa frowned, "I don't want to take that job. I suspect it will be time-consuming. We have so much to do here; I don't need more responsibility."

Ma laughed, "You know what God wants you to do, right? You are being your typical mule-headed, stubborn self again. You had better repent of your attitude before you talk to Joe. Now hurry before you anger God with your stubbornness."

Pa looked at his wife with his mouth wide open. Ma gently tugged at his sleeve before saying, "Come on, quit dawdling."

Pa turned and went down to the furnace room. "God, my wife is right. I am being stubborn. I am sorry and ask for your forgiveness." A quiet, warm glow filled Pa, confirming what he knew to do.

Pa walked through the rain to the bank. As he entered, he looked like a drowned rat, water dripping from his hat and coat. Like all the frontiersmen, he ignored the mud on his boots. Later, Joe would shovel out what Pa and all the others tracked in. He used the soil in his garden, which grew exceptional vegetables from all the fertilizer it contained.

"Joe, I have thought about the director job and think I can do it. Sign me up."

"Thank you. We have what we need to get started since selling the initial stock. I am ready to meet with a state official next week to begin the paperwork. I'll let you know what happens."

Pa walked over to the supply store to chat with Orney.

"Look what the cat drug in." Orney reached out to shake Pa's hand.

"What is the latest around these parts?" Pa already knew, but the customary greeting and small talk still needed to be made.

"Not much, although I believe we are having a heavy dew." Both men chuckled at the old ritual joke.

"Orney, I hear you got talked into something."

"I did at that. How about you?"

"Same. What are we getting into?"

Orney smiled, "I think they call it progress. Our little village is growing, and it is time to take the next step. I know it is hard launching into the unknown, but everyone has stepped out into scary things, and now it is time to do it again. We can help each other more with our bank, instead of relying on those pompous city people. You know how you can't simply talk to someone. You have to ask the receptionist for permission to talk with their secretary to see if Mr. Big Shot has time for you. They are happy to take our money but unhappy when we need help."

Pa nodded, and the conversation turned to the latest in horse tackle.

On the way home, Pa carefully considered his situation. He had plenty of money; perhaps this could be one way to help neighbors. The peaceful, gentle drizzle comforted him as he entered his home. He paused to watch the rain dripping from the hose roof and wondered if the bank could be like the roof, protecting the residents from wet weather. *Roofs do more than keep us dry. They protect us from the sun and heat in summer and cold and snow in the winter.*

Pa wandered into the furnace room and told the furnace everything that had happened. This heavy thinking was new to Pa, and he wasn't sure how to react. The furnace couldn't respond but felt good about this new adventure and was confident Pa would be at the center of village life. It looked forward to Pa telling it everything.

The bank was chartered and soon opened for business. They answered questions and elected directors at the first shareholder meeting. Pa's election was unanimous.

"Mr. Furnace, I was hoping my bank job was over. I want to farm, not do paperwork. I barely know how to read my bills, much less this complicated legal mumbo-jumbo. Yet, everyone wants me to be a part of this experiment. God had better help me, or I will fail spectacularly and take my neighbor's money with me."

Thus began Pa's business career. The shareholders reelected Pa several times as the bank grew from a few notes and a little cash in a safe to an institution with several employees and secure facilities. Along the way, the bank made sure to help young men get started, loaning money to buy cattle and horses. The farmers still worked together like they always did. Now, the business that used to go to the city bank stayed in the village.

Pa never enjoyed his banker duties but looked upon them as service to the village. Eventually, he decided it was time for a younger man to take his place. He kept his stock, passing it to his children after his death.

8

CHOLERA

EVERYONE, EXCEPT THE YOUNGEST SON, WAS UP, STARTING THEIR DAY with breakfast before doing chores. Ma vainly tried waking him.

"Pa, he's dead!"

Pa rushed to the bedroom. On his way, he touched the toasty radiator. It wasn't cold outside, but he needed to satisfy himself that they had heat.

"Luis, quickly, go get the doctor," Pa nearly screamed. The doctor was new in town and spent his time delivering babies, tending to the sick, and fixing broken limbs. He serviced people and animals, getting more business from sick horses than sick people.

On his way back, Luis stopped at the church and, panicked, asked the preacher to come. The sun was peeking above the horizon when he woke the minister. The preacher dressed and grabbed a piece of bread as he left. The two preoccupied men couldn't notice the light snow, making everything look peaceful in the early morning light. Their hurried footsteps crunched in the snow, and their breath made puffs in the morning air. They arrived at the house a few minutes after the doctor.

The whole family followed the doctor into the bedroom. He could see the pain in the parent's eyes and fear in the youngest ones'. They were too young to know what was happening, only that it was terrible, and their family was distraught. The preacher went to Pa and silently put his hand on his shoulder, but Pa never noticed.

"How long was he ill?" The doctor asked.

"He was acting normal yesterday; he didn't go to bed early."

"Anyone else sick?"

All the other children shook their heads, as did the parents.

The doctor examined the body, checking the torso and looking in the eyes and ears while struggling to be professional. *These people are depending on me for answers,* he thought. *I wish I had some.*

"We can't be sure, but I think it's cholera." *Maybe they don't know much about cholera, and it suffices. After all, the child is dead, and the diagnosis is unimportant,* the doctor thought.

"Cholera!" Pa looked confused, his brow deeply furrowed. "How did he get that?"

"Hard to say. I've heard of people getting it from birds or farm animals. Do you have any sick pigs? They usually get cholera if people do."

"No, not yet, at least. Mae, any chickens sick?"

"No, sir."

The doctor looked at each child's tongue and eyes, felt their foreheads, and gave them the best medical exam possible in this frontier town. He did the same to the parents, never sure what he might be looking for but recognizing the fear in each one.

"Well, we must take precautions. This disease is very contagious and could wipe out the village. I am recommending quarantining your farm. You should stay inside as much as possible, only going out to tend to your animals and do essential farm work. We can lift the quarantine in three weeks if no one else gets sick and your pigs stay healthy.

"Let me know if anyone else gets sick. In the meantime, we should quickly bury the body so the disease doesn't spread. Also, burn the bedding and all the child's clothing.

"Finally, wash frequently, before you eat and after you come in from chores. Do you have enough lye soap?"

Ma's voice trembled, "Yes, I made plenty."

The doctor rose and was gone. As he walked down the porch steps, the preacher stopped him. They briefly talked before the preacher nodded and then reentered.

The doctor began thinking as he trudged back to his office; *I told them things they could do that might help and wouldn't hurt. Nothing will help that child, but they shouldn't feel powerless. Even doing worthless things will help them. I wish it were a simple bone to set or a cow having trouble delivering a calf. I know what to do then.*

"I am so sorry." The pastor told the family. There wasn't much else he could say, so he said nothing.

The little family could only sit in shock. Pa knew they couldn't give the child a proper burial. "Could we bury him, then have the funeral later?"

The preacher tenderly responded, "I think that's the right thing to do. I'll show you where to make the grave. I need to leave."

Pa dug another grave near Oscar's. The preacher brought a little cross and said a short prayer before Pa went home. Ma met him at the door.

"Pa, another one died after you left, and the other's acting funny. I think they're sick as well."

Pa rushed in, but it was too late. Whatever cholera was, it was fast. His three youngest were gone.

Again, Pa sent Luis for the doctor and the preacher, and they both said the same things. The doctor left, hanging his head, wishing he knew what to do. Pa buried his sons next to the youngest and slowly stumbled back to his house. His shoulders slumped, and his gait was crooked. Finally, he reached the house, and everyone ate before bed. No one said anything, each grieving in their unique way.

Pa went down to the furnace the following morning.

"Time to feed you again. You're always hungry." The dry wood soon burst into flame, and the evaporating sap quietly whistled. The furnace was, however, apprehensive about the day.

Pa called to Luis when he reached the dining room. "Hey, Luis, time to roll."

"Pa, I don't feel very well. May I sleep a little longer?"

Ma rushed to his room and immediately felt his forehead. "Pa, the boy's burning up! What should we do?"

"In the old country, we put snow in an old rag and lay it on their foreheads. Gustav said it drew the sickness out. I don't know; I don't know."

"Well, we're going to try it. I am not standing by to watch another child die without doing something."

Ma ran outside, scraped a handful of snow into a rag, folded it, and laid it on Luis' forehead. Before long, the snow had melted, but Ma quickly returned with another. She folded more quilts on her son while soothingly speaking, "You can sweat the sickness into the snow."

Luis' thrashed in delirium. He saw wolves, the Barron, and other apparitions trying to destroy him. He, in his feverish fog, resolved they would not take him without a fight, and his frantic moans became, at times, a screeching scream that made everyone in the house cringe.

Luis drifted into a troubled sleep the following day. Ma stayed close in her uncomfortable straight-back chair. Through the night, she kept replacing the melted snow with fresh. Luis continued sleeping all day and the next night. The following morning, he asked for breakfast and started drinking water again. His crisis was past, but Pa's was not.

"Mr. Furnace, I did all I could for my family. I don't know what I could have done differently. Yet, sickness claimed three more and almost got Luis as well. I'm glad Edith and Herman are not living here."

The furnace warmed the room to a comforting temperature. Something let Pa know that there wasn't anything anyone could have done. Somehow, he gained a quiet peace from his visit with the furnace, although he knew the peace came from a different, much more powerful source.

He walked up and hugged his wife. "There wasn't anything we could have done. The Master still loves us."

It took another week before Luis could work outside and two more before the doctor lifted the quarantine. Luis tired quickly, and it was nearly spring before his strength returned. They had the three funerals in the parlor, filled with all their friends and neighbors. Edith cried while her husband hugged her and vainly tried comforting her.

The neighbors were all supportive, yet it was different. Their greetings became awkward, filled with confusion. At first, they didn't want to be around Pa or his family, fearing the disease.

Orney greeted a couple of farmers a few days after the funeral.

"Shame about those three kids. So young and all at once." The conversation quickly turned to the only news in town.

"Yes, it is. And the oldest was sick as well, although he recovered."

"I wonder what it was. The doctor said cholera or something like that. I heard cholera comes from water contaminated with animal waste in it. Is that true?"

"Probably. I don't know. Never heard of it in these parts until now."

The newest resident chimed in, "You want to know what I think? I think the Barron's wizard cursed them for leaving."

Every farmer turned to see who would make such an outlandish claim.

"Hosneck, there ain't no such thing as a curse. And if it was, then why did the Barron wait this long? He's likely dead by now anyway." Orney's upset emotions at Hosneck's gossip made the rest of the men laugh, albeit uncomfortably.

"Well, it has to be something spiritual. We haven't had cholera around here ever. Maybe the old man's a murderer, and fate is finally catching up with him."

"Hosneck, where do you get such ideas? He's a fine man. We can't ask for a better neighbor. Ever since his baby died, why, he's a changed man. Look how many of us he helped and did not accept money for his labor. Would you be like that?"

"Humph. I don't know. It must be something." Hosneck wasn't giving up.

"You're not making sense."

"Yeah? What about those sheep that something killed three days ago? That looked like devil worship to me."

"Hosneck, please! You know wolves got those sheep. Shem even saw one with a sheep part."

Hosneck snorted and shook his head. "You people just don't know, do you?"

Pa strode into the store. "Hello, neighbors. How are things on your side of the fence?"

"Fine. Good to see you." They all responded at once, then fell silent and began studying the floor. Pa looked at them for a minute, then turned to Orney. "I need a new ax."

Orney, glad to do something besides pretend to be interested in harness prices, pulled a couple from a corner. "What do you have in mind? This double-edged one has a nice heft, and this other one's better for splitting wood."

"I think I want the double-edged ax. That way, I won't have to stop to sharpen as often." Pa paid and quietly left.

"Now, what'll he want with that ax? None of us are safe anymore." Hosneck was on a roll.

Hosneck was new to the village, working for the railroad and claiming to be passing through. He made it plain his job often required him to leave for a week or two every couple of months, after which he returned to stay at Mabel's boarding house. No one saw him work, which fed rumors that he was an outlaw using the tiny village as a hideout. He never told anyone his first name and only went by Hosneck. Some thought they heard him say someone could curse him if they knew his full name.

If anyone had the patience to talk with him for more than a few minutes, they quickly discovered that he was brilliant. Some said his strange ways were the result of his intelligence. He liked to be the center of attention, and no one saw him in church. He was not shy about his spiritual side, claiming to have studied in exotic places like Pittsburg, Miami, and the Egyptian pyramids. No one knew what he believed, and he changed his mind frequently.

Hosneck was a small man with ragged, unkempt hair and a beard that was neither full nor clean-shaven, making him look dirty. He had a strange walk, tilting to one side with each step, claiming it was from an injury received while building a railroad tunnel. His eyes constantly darted from one thing to another. He never looked anyone in the eye, and his hands were always in motion whether he was talking or not. Some claimed they could see either words or symbols faintly written on his beat-up wide-brim hat. Others said it was only folds and creases because he always wore it. He constantly muttered strange sounds, sometimes clucking like a chicken as he walked, and every morning, he crowed like a rooster at the rising sun. A speech impediment made him hiss like a snake when he talked. Even in this frontier area, villagers said he had an offensive smell. His mottled brown teeth, with some missing, gave him a wild appearance. People watched him closely since he tended to borrow things not his, even though he had more money than anyone.

Most people didn't want to associate with him but were too polite to say anything. Regardless, Hosneck's different ways entertained people in this sleepy village and gave them something to talk about.

The rest of the conversation centered on why Pa might need a new ax.

A few weeks later, Ma approached Pa. "It's very strange. The church ladies aren't including me in their projects. I wonder why?"

"They may think you need time to yourself and don't want to impose. It'll be okay." Pa was encouraging as he rose to hug Ma.

"I don't know. It seems like everyone treats us like we're vermin. You think it might be because of cholera?"

"Could be. No one wants to get that sick. Wait awhile; our neighbors are good people and will come around."

He's so different. He would have become furious in times past. He's still stubborn, but stubborn in a good way. I think I like the new Pa. Ma marveled to herself about her husband's change, as she often did.

Sunday, the preacher visited after church. Pa seldom missed a church service except when their house was under quarantine. They sat in the parlor and talked. Or rather, the family talked, and the preacher listened. He heard their grief over their young sons and knew better than to try answering their "whys." Everyone enjoyed the apple pie that Mae served. The furnace listened carefully, wanting to comfort them somehow. It consoled itself by ensuring the house was as warm as it could make it.

Michael, the preacher's next-door neighbor, liked talking with the preacher, who was the only one who seemed to have the time for Michael. Michael was a good man but the least intelligent in the village. He was single and, truth be known, was afraid of women and avoided them at every opportunity. Everyone adopted him, hiring him to do odd jobs and farm work and generally looking after him. Michael was a slow worker, careful to do his job, often more in the way than helpful. Today, he began walking with the preacher on their way home.

"Hey, Mr. Preacher, whatcha been doing?"

"Well, Michael, I visited our friends, the Schumerhass. It's a tragedy about their children."

"Yes, they looked like fine boys. Too bad."

As they walked, enjoying their silent fellowship, a flock of crows flew out of weeds on the side of the ditch, scared by a yapping dog. The dog herded the crows toward the men, forcing them to duck. It happened in a heartbeat, but the startled preacher stumbled as he ducked.

"Ow! I twisted my ankle. Help me home, will you?"

Michael helped lift the preacher to his good foot, then supported him as they hobbled toward the preacher's house. They were almost there when Hosneck scurried up.

'What happened?"

"I was returning from visiting the Schumerhass when a dog flushed some crows. The birds startled me, and I twisted my ankle when I stumbled."

"I knew it. Those people put a devil's hex on you, Preacher. Crows always do evil spirits' work!" Honeck's lisp always became more pronounced when he was excited.

"Now Hosneck, there's no such thing as hexes, and those kind people wouldn't hex anything even if they could. Don't be spreading such lies!"

"Ha! They're talking to their dead boys, getting them to do evil. That's what it is. We had all better watch our step." Hosneck couldn't wait to return to the supply store with his new revelation.

"Brother Hosneck, Jesus is my Lord, and He's more than able to protect me, even if someone could throw a hex. Maybe you should turn to Jesus yourself, and then you wouldn't see demons in every bird."

"They're there all right. I'm mixing more camphor potion to keep them from hexing my food! I don't want to choke on anything. You should, too."

Hosneck turned and ran to the store while the preacher hobbled into his house, shaking his head.

"Preacher, you sure about them not putting hexes on people?" Michael was worried.

"I'm sure. I can't understand what got into Hosneck, him saying those nasty things about such good people."

"But there have been a lot of bad things happening—those sheep, for instance. Then Henry's roof started leaking, and Fredrick's potatoes rotted! What're we going to do?" Michael wrung his hands as he talked.

"We aren't doing anything. Wolves have always taken a few sheep, all roofs leak eventually and need repairs, and Fredrick's potatoes were two years old! If they hadn't rotted, something might be wrong. It's okay." The preacher tried to be reassuring, but his sore ankle made it difficult.

"I don't know…" Michael's voice trailed off.

The next day, Pa went into the village to buy coal. He noticed the people immediately moved out of his way as he drove down the street, and suddenly, everyone in the supply store found urgent business elsewhere. Orney seemed preoccupied when Pa asked about coal.

"It's in the back. Load your wagon like normal, and you can pay on the way out."

"What's going on? No one wants to talk with me, even say hello. Orney was as rude as I have ever seen him. Must be an election coming up, with everyone mad at everyone else." Pa muttered to his horses as he loaded his wagon.

After unloading his coal and finishing his chores, Pa sat on his log next to the furnace.

"I don't understand, Mr. Furnace. They used to be so friendly to us, and now it's like we carry the plague." The reservoir water temperature was nearly perfect, causing Pa to adjust the airflow.

The furnace dimmed its fire slightly, sad for Pa and his family. It sensed everyone in the house was depressed and isolated. Mae hurt more than the others. She felt like a mother to her little brothers and now grieved their loss in her deepest parts, softly crying at night. The furnace heard her through the radiators, but there was nothing it nor anyone could do.

Pa, Ma, Luis, and Mae ate their supper in depressed silence. Finally, Mae asked, "May I be excused? I'm exhausted and want to go to bed."

The wind picked up, making a low, howling noise in the orchard. Mae huddled under her covers, emotionally exhausted, knowing she couldn't hide in Edith's bed. Eventually, Mae fell asleep, but then the nightmares started. A giant headless ghost chicken chased her and her little brothers everywhere. She couldn't escape it, and her legs wouldn't run. Frozen, she saw the monstrosity laugh as it captured her brothers' heads, then began chasing her for her head. In terror, she screamed, not a normal scream, but the blood-curdling scream of a desperate woman, knowing the terror of losing her life in the most horrible way possible. She bolted upright in bed and kept screaming, her eyes scrunched tightly closed, and her fists clenched, not realizing she was awake.

Pa raced up the stairs and into Mae's room, followed by Ma and Luis. "What's wrong?" But Mae was so frightened she couldn't stop screaming as loud as she could. Sweat poured from her forehead.

Ma sat on the bed and hugged her terrified daughter. "It's okay. It was only a dream. We don't need to be afraid of our dreams. You're safe now. Look, I'll stay with you tonight. You'll be safe." The distressed furnace was glad Ma could comfort the girl while wishing it could do something. Mae gradually calmed down, her screams becoming spasmatic gulps of air that shook her frame.

Michael happened to be returning from his traps in the forest and was walking past the Schumerhass' house when Mae started screaming. Her terror infected Michael, who immediately ran into the village.

The following day, he went to the supply store, where the men were again solving the world's problems, particularly corn prices, when Michael burst in.

"I heard it. I really did. It was a haunt, I tell you, a real haunt. Last night, I returned from checking my traps, and right by the Schumerhass' house, the haunt started screaming and chasing me. It was awful! It wanted my soul and would've taken it right there! No matter what, I'm not going past that house at night again!"

Orney listened, wanting to stop gossip, "Now Michael, it's all right. There's nothing to fear. You walked past that house many times, in both the full moon and the dark, and nothing happened."

"But this is the first time since the haunt took those boys." By mid-afternoon, everyone in the village heard the story. Each retelling made the haunt more fearsome, dragging chains or something worse.

Several young boys thought it might be fun to see for themselves. They crept along the road that night, carefully keeping in the shadows. They waited near the Schumerhass' home, hoping and fearing they might see the haunt. Each secretly terrified child mentally prayed for nothing to happen but didn't dare let the others know how afraid he was. They needed to "outbrave" each other.

Mae stayed up as late as she could, fearfully watching out the windows. Eventually, she went to bed and burrowed deep into her covers. Again, the grief of losing her brothers overcame her as she drifted into a troubled sleep. This time, there were many ghost chickens, all looking for heads. She tried running, but something tangled her feet, and she couldn't move. She screamed, all the horror of her dream burst forth, exactly like the previous night.

Like before, her mother rushed to comfort her, followed by her father and brother. With effort, they managed to wake and quiet Mae. Ma again reassured Mae she would stay the night.

The boys heard Mae's screams. They stopped and stared at the oversized house, made more prominent by the moonlight. The youngest child panicked first, turned, and started running, screaming, "Mama! Help!" The boy's fears catalyzed the others to race home.

"It was huge! It almost caught me! I could feel its icy breath on my neck." Before long, every family heard a different version of the adventure, becoming increasingly terrifying with each retelling.

The next day, the oldest boy teased the youngest about his fear, jumping and screaming from behind a bush. The boy ran as fast as he could, looking over his shoulder while the other laughed. The running boy tripped and fell into a ditch, crying in terror, while the tormentor quickly ran away, knowing he was in trouble.

The injured child's mother rushed out. "What happened?" Immediately, she saw the child's arm hanging unnaturally. She scooped him up and brought him to the doctor, who set the broken arm. He hated fixing children's bones; they didn't understand and consequently screamed terribly.

The commotion again attracted Hosneck's attention as he loitered in the supply store. He wandered out into the street and saw the injured with his mother.

"What happened?"

"My child fell and broke his arm. He needs to be more careful."

"It was the haunt. I heard it and had to run for my life. It almost got me this time." The child already started bragging about the adventure.

"In broad daylight? That's a powerful haunt, for sure." Hosneck had more ammunition.

Pa didn't say much as he and his family finished their daily chores. Finally, as night was getting close, Pa took Ma's hand. "I don't know what I should do. It is best if you stay with Mae tonight. Wake her as soon as the nightmares start. I'll be back when I'll be back." And Pa was gone.

He walked to the church, usually left open. Overcome, he prostrated at the front, weeping and softly talking to God. The preacher was about to go home and decided not to disturb the giant man on the floor.

Pa quietly called to Jesus, "What do I do?" His prayer was simple, only asking for Pa's next step. Later, Pa would speak about how difficult it was to pray. His prayers felt like they bounced off a stone wall before colliding with him. Between his cries for help, Pa confessed every sin he had committed or thought of committing. He confessed his humanity and helplessness. He repeatedly told the Lord that the Lord was the ruler of everything. His tears wet the church floor. In every way he could, Pa humbled himself.

The following day, the preacher looked inside the church. As far as he could tell, Pa had not moved. He was still softly crying to God, covering his head with his hands. Quietly, he left Pa alone with his Lord, not knowing what else to do.

Pa stayed on the floor all day until mid-afternoon when he rose.

"Thank you, Lord. I think I know what to do now."

He called his family together before he even took his coat off. They had already finished eating, but Pa's food would wait.

"Mae, these nightmares, they're not right. Do you believe Jesus can take them?"

"I don't know, Pa, they're so real."

"Well, He can. We're going to ask Him to do that. Can you trust Him for His help?"

"I can try." Mae's upper lip trembled as her tears gently touched her cheeks. She shook her head, struggling to focus on Jesus instead of the vivid memories of her dreams.

Pa cleared his throat. "Jesus, we know You love us, and You love Mae. We know we can't do anything about these dreams, but You can. Please take these dreams away from Mae, give her a good night's sleep, and replace the fear with thoughts of Your love. Thank you, Jesus, our Lord."

Mae suddenly snapped to attention, stiffing her back, looking up, and smiling broadly. "I feel so free! They're gone! I am not afraid of any ghost chickens!" She hopped as if she were five years old again.

Pa straightened up and turned to Ma. "I'm hungry. I think I've worked harder today than I ever have. We got any supper?"

Mae never again dreamed of the ghost chicken and only thought about it when she wanted to tell how much Jesus had done for her.

The next day, Pa found the preacher and told him what had happened. The two bowed their heads, and the preacher thanked Jesus for caring for Mae.

"Friend, it seems that there're a lot of rumors floating around town. Rumors that you're putting hexes on people, causing bad things to happen. People aren't telling me much because they know I don't believe in hexes, but they're whispering to each other."

Pa nodded. "I know what I must do. I know what the problem is and how to solve it." And then he was gone.

Nearly everyone in town crowded around Hosneck, listening to what he had to say when Pa arrived at the supply store. Pa only heard Hosneck say something about a haunt, and the townsfolk needed to do something about it before Pa sprang into action.

He pushed into the crowd and lifted the gossip by his coat with one hand. His roar, once again sounding like a cross between a bull and a wounded bear, silenced everyone. No one wanted to get near those massive arms holding Hosneck.

"You saying bad things about me and my family?"

Hosneck struggled to free himself. "Let me go. I haven't done anything."

Hosneck's feeble protests enraged Pa even more, turning his deep voice into an even more frightening, intense, menacing growl. Later, the people would claim Pa's voice was so loud it rattled windows across the street. "You're an evil little man, turning good neighbors against each other. Why? For sport?"

With one arm, Pa carried Hosneck to the door and tossed him into the street like one tosses a wormy apple to a hog. Before Hosneck could rise, Pa lifted him again with one arm, this time high over his head. Hosneck watched in horror as Pa brought his other massive fist back, preparing to strike. Hosneck only had time for one thought: *He'll kill me if he hits me.*

After what felt like an eternity, a woman cried desperately, "Don't do it, Pa. He's not worth it."

Pa paused, turned while holding Hosneck in the air, and looked at his wife. Indecision plagued his mind, and he started twirling his mustache. Hosneck began pleading for his life in his whiney, hissing voice, "Please, I'm sorry. I don't know why I said those things. Please, let me go."

"Pa, two wrongs don't make a right. Jesus wouldn't like it if you hit him, although we both know he deserves it and worse. Please don't!" Ma grabbed her husband's arm as she pleaded.

By now, the entire town had surrounded the two men. Most wanted Pa to hit Hosneck as hard as possible and were secretly glad to hear the rascal whimper.

Pa turned and stared long at Hosneck before growling another low, frightening growl, "I should do you in for what you have done to me, even in my time of great grief." Pa effortlessly tossed him towards the train station as if he were discarding garbage scrap. "Don't you think it's time for you to find someplace else to live? I don't want to skin you and nail your sorry hide to a signpost as they did to scoundrels like you in the old country."

"I'm leaving on the next train. You don't have to worry about me; I'm going!" Relief flooded Hosneck as he, trembling, rose and scurried to the station. He left on the afternoon train, and no one in the village saw him again.

As Hosneck scampered from the street, the entire town cheered and applauded. Ma rushed to Pa's side, "I'm so proud of you! You did the right thing."

Pa could hear snippets of different neighbors' conversations.

"I never believed what Hosneck said."

"No such thing as a Haunt."

"Glad that pest's gone."

"Whoever heard of hexes anyways."

That night, Pa sat in his spot in the furnace room. "Mr. Furnace, isn't it strange how people act? They're your friends until they aren't. Everything'll take a while to return to how they were, but in the meantime, I will treat everyone the best I can."

The furnace showed its approval with a pop and a burst of sparks.

9

SICK

BEFORE ANYONE REALIZED HOW QUICKLY THE SEASONS AND YEARS PASS, Luis and Mae married exceptional spouses, and Edith had her third child. Luis and his wife, Emma, lived in Pa's house. Their excuse was wanting to be close to their acres. The reality was that he wanted to better care for Luis' parents.

Time began showing on Pa. His hair disappeared except for a white fringe, most of his teeth fell out, and his strength diminished. He never admitted he couldn't see well and spoke louder in his booming voice that rattled the dishes.

"Pa, the Chang family has another child."

"What did you say? Don't mumble. Everyone always mumbles, and they don't tell me things. I don't know why you people mistreat me so badly." Pa grumbled, but everyone knew it was his hearing loss. His stubbornness kept him working, but Ma could see he took longer to do the same task and rested often. Luis struggled to help without offending him. The little village also changed, growing and adding new services, such as a blacksmith, post office, boarding house, and an undertaker. The blacksmith, who was even stronger than Pa, was also the village dentist. His incredible strength allowed him to pull infected teeth easily.

Orney finally succumbed to the years, leaving his oldest son, Cas, to manage the store. His other children started farms nearby, clearing trees, making pastures, and building homes. Pa often sat in the furnace room, meditating on the changes since Oscar hired him ages ago. Just as Orney was his best friend, Cas was Luis' best friend. Pa welcomed the furnace's extra heat in colder weather.

"Mr. Furnace, it's lonely now. All my friends have died. There is no one left close to my age. I don't belong here. I am a fugitive, lost from a time that no longer exists. I guess it will soon be my turn to go. But Mr. Furnace, you are still here and always listen to me. I like coming down here. You warm my bones when I sit next to you. I feel like my fire is going out."

Pa's little speech saddened the furnace. It tried to warm the room a little more for the old giant. *I don't feel so good myself. I wonder if it is getting close to my fires going out and if the family will replace me. That time has to come.*

The year Orney died saw poor crops. Wet Spring weather delayed the fieldwork. Then, a drought ravaged the newly planted crops, stunting the sprouting plants. Heavy rains as the wheat ripened saved the corn crop but caused moldy wheat. At first, the alfalfa grew enough that the first cutting filled half the mow. Then, in the drought, the alfalfa turned brown and died. Giant cracks in the soil appeared, large enough to trip the careless. Several hail storms pounded their crops, especially their garden and the corn.

"Ma, anything that can go wrong has gone wrong this year." It was unusual for Pa to share his concerns.

Pa reluctantly sold most of his livestock to pay bills. "It's for the best," he said, "I don't have enough feed for them in the coming winter." He worried about how much longer he could keep his aging draft horses and didn't have money to replace them.

Winter came early, making things worse. What corn survived the hail didn't have time to fully ripen, with the stalks only fired about a foot above the soil. They harvested a partial crop to feed his remaining animals, with none left for the market.

"Luis, we need to cut more wood. There isn't enough money for coal. Maybe next year will be better. I am thankful I have enough savings in the bank to pay our taxes." Pa tried to be optimistic and make the best of things.

He and Luis cut wood daily, the job made difficult by the severe winter. His furnace needed a lot of fuel under the best conditions, but the windy, cold weather made it difficult to cut enough wood to keep the house warm. This winter was one of the coldest and windiest anyone remembered. The deeply buried water line from the windmill froze, forcing them to carry buckets of water for their horses and their few remaining livestock.

"Luis, I am so glad we put that pump and well inside the house. The furnace keeps the water from freezing," Pa commented during supper one night.

"Well, I wish we had heat in the outhouse," Ma muttered under her breath. Luis only smiled.

The cold and heavy snow made cutting firewood so challenging that they began cutting the trees closest to the house to get what fuel they could, even using fence row brush. Where oak stood for decades, now pines and other softwood trees stood, soon falling before their axes and saws to feed the ever-hungry furnace.

"Luis, we need so much fuel that we don't have time to let this wood dry. I hope it burns all right. I remember Orney telling me not to use so much softwood and especially brush, but a man must do what he must."

"Yes, Pa."

Ma and Luis knew how hard it was to fuel the furnace. They saved fuel by closing most of the second-story room. The furnace knew they struggled and did the best it could. The family finally made it through most of the winter and awaited spring's arrival.

The furnace didn't feel good. It felt congested and lonely since Pa didn't spend as much time with it; instead, he took long naps under a pile of comforters. But, like a good soldier, the furnace did its best to warm the family. The wood made lots of ash, forcing Pa to clean it several times each day only to see the ash bin quickly fill. The ash restricted airflow, making the increasingly inefficient furnace sneeze into the chimney and eat even more wood. The chimney always bellowed thick, black smoke that smelled.

It was starting to warm but still cold in April, almost Easter, when Edith, looking towards her parents' house, saw an inferno erupt from the housetop. A stream of molten fire burst from the chimney, and flaming blobs of creosote fell from the geyser, igniting the roof. A deep roar increased in volume as the fire fountain reached ever higher. The furnace tried to stop belching fire but couldn't.

"Go to every neighbor and get help. Tell them to bring buckets. Pa's house is on fire, and we must save it!" Her oldest ran to neighbors, pounding doors, yelling, and pointing at Pa's house. Men and women grabbed buckets and rushed to the Schumerhass' home. Meanwhile, Edith raced to Pa's door, screaming, and got her brother, his wife, and her parents out of the house. By now, everyone in the village could see, and many could hear the chimney fire.

Pa raced to the basement and immediately shoveled ash into the firebox to smother the furnace fire. He then closed the firebox and the ash bin, minimizing airflow. As he did, the fire jet began dying down, reducing the burning cresol carried from the chimney. The roar became a rumble before gradually stopping, but only after all the chimney cresol had burned out.

Pa ran back to the first floor and pumped water into his bucket. A neighbor pushed another bucket into its place after each pail was full. Soon, everyone handed buckets of water from the pump through a window and handed them up a ladder to men on the burning roof. Others tried smothering flames with blankets. Luis saw Pa's exhaustion and unceremoniously pushed him from the pump handle, knowing he would apologize later. Women started bringing everything they could from the house to the road, trying to save furniture, bedding, and clothing.

Falling embers from the unstable roof set attic beams and decking on fire. Someone chopped through the roof's remains with an ax before jumping into the attic, allowing easier access for the water buckets. Extinguished but molten cresol oozed into cracks, dripping unseen into the outside walls before re-igniting. The men followed the fire's glow, chopping into attic walls as needed to throw water on burning timber.

The firefighters finally decided the inferno was out. The villagers had extinguished the roof blaze, and the chimney no longer spouted flames. They couldn't see any fire in the attic and began putting their buckets away.

One of the young boys, usually more underfoot than helpful, leaned against a wall on the second floor. "Hey, this is *hot!*" His exclamation brought the attention of several adults, one of whom chopped a hole into the wall. Flames exploded from the cavity, causing him to jump back.

They restarted the bucket brigade, cutting holes and splashing water inside every wall. They continued until everyone was satisfied the fire was indeed out. This time, it was.

Once the crisis passed, Ma collapsed in a chair on the road with her head in her hands. The preacher's wife stood beside her, with her hand on Ma's shoulder. Pa stood on the corduroy road, looking sorrowfully at the char that was the remains of his house's second floor, trying hard not to cry. The smoke had blackened the exhausted neighbors, and several had their eyebrows singed. They stood in a daze, unsure what to do or say, until Cas stood on a nearby wagon and motioned for quiet.

"Neighbors, we have a problem. Mr. Schumerhass is one of our best friends, always willing to help each of us no matter what the problem was. It's been a bad year for all of us, but if we pitch in, we can rebuild this house and get it done before the fields are ready to work in. Who's with me to help our neighbor?"

There was a general shout of assent. Galvanized once more, the village men raced to get tools. Most returned with a few sticks of lumber and siding. Cas donated several caskets of nails for the siding. *He's much more generous than his father*, thought Pa.

The men dismantled the roof, attic, and second floor, discovering the fires in the walls were worse than expected. The sobering shock of realizing how close they came to losing the house gave everyone pause. *If this house had collapsed while we were inside fighting that fire, I don't see how some of us would have got out alive*, thought Cas.

Edith approached her father. "We decided you must stay with us until you finish rebuilding the house. We don't have much room nor the conveniences you have, but we'll manage."

The frontier men were all handy with their tools, having built the town's structures. They sorted the salvaged lumber into piles for reuse and scrap, which would become furnace fuel. Several men headed to the forest and returned with oak trees to shape into beams. The farmers expertly used their braces and bits to prepare the new beams for pegs. Younger children pulled nails from siding and straightened the best for reuse, while the women went home to return with food. Somehow, the townspeople turned the tragedy into a community party, working and joking and everyone having a good time. Pa marveled at everyone knowing what to do without anyone directing the project.

"Once we have placed the window frames, I'll measure them and get new windows for you. When we finish, your second story will have the best windows in the house." Cas told Pa.

Over the next three weeks, the men rebuilt the second floor and attic. "I think we should deck the roof instead of only using lathe for shingles," Shem suggested. "That way, you'll have a stronger roof."

They had enough lumber between the donated material and Pa's stockpile. Pa had continued Oscar's tradition and had more than enough shingles for the entire roof. Fortunately, all the radiators, piping, and inside water well were undamaged, as was the food in the cellar.

Pa examined the fire-damaged chimney, observing the soot and partially burned cresol coating the inside. Luis filled a burlap feed bag with gravel and, using a rope, cleaned the chimney by running it up and down the inside. Years before, Pa had installed a metal clean-out port at the chimney base, which they now used to remove the fallen residue. Unfortunately, Pa could see the badly damaged brick.

Cas disappeared, then returned with a catalog. "Look, we can install a heavy metal pipe inside the brick. It'll act like the chimney and won't have all the brick edges for cresol to catch on. If we use these spacers, we can keep it away from the brick, and circulating air will keep it from deteriorating. This top gadget lets the smoke out but won't let rain in."

Pa looked at the picture and, not understanding, nodded. *How will I pay for this? Should I apply for a loan from our little bank?*

"I think I can have it here in a couple of days. Don't use the furnace until then. And don't worry; I will give you credit." Cas disappeared but left his enthusiasm. The men made what brick repairs they could, but it was clear it wasn't enough.

It only took a little more than two weeks before they could move back home. The house had different noises, especially where the men patched the new second floor to the old first, but they were home. While sad about the damage he caused, the furnace felt very loved as his family and their friends made repairs.

Pa cautiously started a small fire in the furnace before rushing outside to watch the chimney. Smoke billowed from under the new chimney cap, but everything else looked like it should. Returning, he built a fire to last the evening. Somehow, he found enough money to buy a load of coal.

The furnace and everyone else in the house felt better after the fire started. Pa and Luis thanked each neighbor, embarrassing most with their gratitude.

The next evening, Pa sat on his block and talked to the furnace.

"Well, my friend. You surely didn't feel good. That was a real scare. I learned pine is too much for you, and the sap sticks to the chimney wall. I'll be more careful from now on and feed you better."

Pa looked in the ash bin, then started shoveling ash. He gave the grate level a couple of quick pulls, but this time, when he looked in the ash bin, he saw a lot of burning wood.

"Wha, what's this? Your grates have burned through. I'll have to see if I can get more tomorrow. It looks like it'll be okay for the evening; I'll build a small fire. Ma will understand, although she won't like it one bit."

The furnace was embarrassed. It felt better, but still sick. The grates kept the fire in the firebox while allowing ash to drop into the ash bin. It was normal for the grates to fail every few years. The furnace felt sick everywhere. It didn't understand its problems, much less how to tell Pa.

The next day, Pa entered the supply store. "Hello, Cas. Hope you're having a good day."

"Better than I deserve, that's for sure. What can I do for you?"

"I need a set of grates for the furnace. It looks like several burned through. If it's not one thing, it's another."

"Let's look in the catalog. Here's your furnace model. These are your grates. You want me to order a set?"

"Yes, please do. But I have a problem. As you know, I don't have any money right now. Can you help me out?"

Cas thought for a moment, then rummaged around his desk. Finally, he pulled a paper from the chaos and spread it on the counter. "I have an order for some timber, cut and squared. If you can get me four beams, each about fifty feet long, we'll call it even, for both the chimney pipe and the grates."

Pa didn't think long. "Deal. I'll start on them today."

"I don't need them for three weeks but will take them when you have them. Meanwhile, I'll place the order."

As soon as Pa entered his house, he grabbed his wife. "Cas will trade grates for oak beams. Can you believe it? We are getting the best of this deal! Cas does more than treat us right."

Then, Pa called to his son, "Luis, we have work to do."

The two men went to the woods, where they felled the giant trees and stripped the smaller branches. Using their draft horses, they pulled the tree back to their buildings. Then, while Pa squared the timber with his broad ax, Luis gathered the limbs for fuel. They wasted nothing.

"I don't remember this job being this hard," Pa thought. "I used to be able to do this all day, but now I have to rest every few minutes."

Pa and Luis needed several days to finish the order. The horses pulled the first beam through the slushy mud to behind the store. "Cas, we have the beams. Where do you want them?" Pa called out.

"That's fine right there. Do you mind coming inside? Here's some hot coffee for both of you."

Cas rummaged around his desk, looking for something important. Then he rummaged on the counter, piled high with catalogs, and finally pulled an envelope from under a stack in one of his desk drawers. "I knew I had it somewhere. Here is the letter from the furnace people. Your grates will take another week to ship and will come by rail. They're cast iron and look heavy. When they come in, I'll help install them. In the meantime, be careful. This town doesn't need more excitement."

Pa and Luis went to drag the rest of the beam order to the store. Luis noticed Pa's struggles and how slowly he moved. That night, Pa slept soundly, his snoring echoing throughout the house. The furnace listened, glad Pa was resting but concerned about how tired he was.

Cas, Luis, and Pa easily installed the grates after they cleaned the firebox. The grates lay on a rocker arm, and their intermeshing fingers matched to hold burning wood and coal. Pa started a fire to test the grates, and they worked well.

The next day, Pa took his wagon into town. He noticed the train station had a pile of old railroad ties waiting for disposal. Apparently, a crew replaced thirty ties when repairing tracks after a derailment. Pa went inside and asked the station master about the ties.

"They're no good to us. Tell you what, I'll give you a penny a tie to haul them off."

Pa returned for Luis, and the two loaded the ties. Back in the house, they used the cross-cut saw to cut the first tie into short lengths. Pa threw the cut tie into the coal bin, then went to the furnace room. He threw one section into the furnace, ensuring the fire had plenty of coal. Unfortunately, long ago, the railroad had started using ties soaked in cresol to slow rotting.

The tie reeked as it burned. The stench rose through the house, making everything smell like burning tree sap. The furnace tried its best to keep the odor inside the firebox, but it couldn't. Downdrafts pushed the black smoke billowing from the chimney towards the barn. The tie burned more intensely than anything Pa had ever seen. Pa kept adjusting the air flow to keep from overheating the water but heard it boiling despite his best efforts.

Moments later, Ma stomped into the furnace room, coughing. "What have you done? This stink is terrible! It'll make us all sick, for sure."

Pa could only look at her, his head hanging and guilt-stricken. "I'm sorry," he finally mumbled.

It took quite a long while for the tie to burn down. "Well, Mr. Furnace. I won't do that again. Was Ma ever mad! I don't blame her. Now I have to carry these ties out of here and hope they don't accidentally get used. I think I can use them to shore up the hog fence. They are rotten but will do for a few years."

10

LUIS

THE FARM BECAME INCREASINGLY PROFITABLE EACH YEAR DUE TO THE family's modernization efforts. They rebuilt their herds and added a few goats. No one remembered when the cats arrived; they quickly controlled the mice and rats in the barns. Without mice, no one saw snakes in the henhouse. Luis noticed he had more feed without the varmints.

"Ma, it looks like things are back on track. I never thought we would be this prosperous. Life was hard in the old country, and we never had much to show for our work."

Luis now did the heavy work, and his children helped just as he had when he was their age. Pa could hardly see or hear and stooped badly. He still insisted on carrying the ashes out, but getting them up the stairs was almost more than he could do. He shuffled rather than walked and seemed cold all the time. His clothes hung like a flag without wind on his gaunt, bony frame. Worse, everything hurt, although he never complained.

The unseasonably warm weather was starting to melt snow one late winter. Pa and Ma still wanted a jacket when outside, but Luis only wanted his heavy work shirt. The alfalfa was still dormant, but the promise of good farming days was in the air. Soon, they would work from daybreak to dusk, but on this evening, the family rested on their porch and enjoyed the sunset. The family listened to the first few migrating birds in the still air. Barn odors and soft animal sounds made a pleasant backdrop.

Luis asked Pa, "Did you ever think your life would turn out like this?"

Pa thought for a minute, "No, I didn't. I only wanted a safe place to live and earn enough to meet our family's humble needs. I wondered what would happen to us when we left the Old Country. It was so hard to get here. Then, we stumbled onto Oscar, and our fortunes turned around. He essentially gave us his farm. We became so prosperous that it went to my head. But, as a result, I was broken when my daughter died. Jesus reached into my hard heart and changed me.

"We installed the furnace, the stove, and the indoor pump. It was a miracle how our neighbors helped dig our basement. Our crops usually did well, as did the vegetable business. Then I worked with the bank, which is now doing very well. It has helped almost everyone in the village.

"It wasn't all perfect, like when the little boys died of cholera. I am not convinced that was what it was, but they are still gone, and it doesn't matter. Luis, we thought we might also lose you, but you were so strong you pulled through. Either that or you were too stubborn to die."

Ma smiled, "Like father, like son."

Pa gave her a dirty look. "We had a few bad years, but most years were good. We sold a lot of timber, which also gave us more farmland.

"I am incredibly proud and humbled by my family. Each of you is special and has done well. The grandkids bring me so much joy. I would never have believed I would live long enough to see this. So many of our neighbors in the Old Country died from many causes before they saw what their families became.

"I am proud of this country. It has treated me fairly, unlike the Barron in the Old Country."

Ma added, "You have done much for your neighbors and the village. You can't sit back if you see someone with a need. I am so proud of you. Look how many neighbors you were a pallbearer for. That speaks to how well the community thinks of you."

Pa smiled, "I think God had his hand in everything that happened to us. He usually worked behind the scenes but sometimes in the open. I know what a difference he made in my life. I won't say I am happier, but rather much more contented. My life is like a cow laying in warm sunshine, chewing its cud, and watching the world. Everything turned out better than I had any right to think, much less deserve. I only wish I had trusted Jesus long before I did. Thinking back, that was a miserable time which I should forget."

The family silently meditated on life until the sun reached the horizon, and then they rose and went to bed.

Pa still talked to his furnace. "Mr. Furnace, how are you this day?" They had replaced numerous grates, yet the furnace didn't feel well; his pipes didn't carry heat like designed, as if something clogged them. Still, his job was to do his best, and that was what he did. But the furnace knew something was wrong with Pa. Every day, the furnace grew more concerned about Pa.

It happened on a brisk spring day. Pa was so tired that he overslept. He checked the furnace firebox before grabbing two pails filled with cold ash and struggling up the stairs. The pails felt heavier than usual, but he stubbornly fought up the stairs, stopping every other step to catch his breath. Usually, he piled ash in a far corner next to the barn, but this day, Pa never got there. Ma found him in the yard, face down, the buckets spilling ash onto the barnyard.

"Luis! Help me with Pa!" she screamed. Pa's face was bright red yet turning a pale gray. His left hand twitched as he clutched his chest, and his eyes rolled back. Luis and Ma carried the frail man back to his bed, where Ma took his shoes off and tucked him under the covers as Luis raced to get the village doctor. Pa was gone before he arrived; Ma held her husband while weeping.

The entire village attended Pa's funeral in the family parlor. The preacher, a young man who took over after the older preacher passed, gave the sermon. Everyone said the right things, adding how much they missed Pa. The furnace wished he could tell everyone how good a friend Pa had been to him, but instead, he consoled himself by listening through the radiators. It knew that perhaps, except for Ma, it would miss Pa more than anyone else. Somehow, the furnace felt responsible for Pa's death; he was carrying its ashes. The neighbors left as husbands and wives agreed the new preacher couldn't do nearly as good a job as the old one.

Luis dug the grave while the preacher pounded the crude cross with Pa's name at the head. They carefully lowered the pine casket before covering it. Every shovel-full was another period ending the sentence of Pa's life. After a prayer, they shook hands, and then Luis slowly stumbled back home, carrying his shovel and not seeing where he went.

Ma met him at the door. "I'm glad Mae and Edith and, of course, you were here. I wish we could have waited for Herman, but we couldn't. Pa got to play with his grandkids and see how his labors prospered. We're so fortunate, Luis. It looks like the farm's yours now. Pa told me that's what he wanted. The others made their way in life and are doing well. We will divide Pa's money and bank stock with the others. That will be a fair distribution, especially since you worked hard on the farm. He was proud of you and your children." Ma's reflections weighed on Luis as he wondered if he was ready for the responsibility. The furnace overheard their conversation and vowed to help Luis all it could.

Luis began instituting his new ideas, which increased his productivity. His twins worked hard but weren't old enough to work long hours. He hired Wolf, a drifter, who stayed in their old pigsty to help with the extra work. Ma insisted that Wolf share their meals and treated him like Oscar treated the refugees many years ago. Wolf was nice enough but wanted to be alone as much as possible. Luis thought he wasn't quite right mentally, but since he did his work and appeared harmless, he was glad to have him.

Ma took to caring for the furnace, and she tightly held that connection to Pa. She didn't ask the furnace for its opinions on life. But she did feed it at least three times a day in cold weather and carried out the ashes. Sometimes, she lingered, reminiscing about her life with Pa. The furnace looked forward to her visits and did its best to keep the house warm.

The seasons came and went until late one chilly morning; the furnace heard Luis call into his mother's bedroom. "Ma, it's late. You okay?" but there was no answer. The preacher held her funeral in the parlor, giving a good sermon; this time, the villagers made no comparison to the preacher's predecessor. The congregation now accepted him.

The farming season was particularly profitable the year Ma passed. The crops yielded more than expected, and the cattle sold for higher prices. Luis' wife, Emma, was particularly contented, cooking on her stove and caring for her family. Only the furnace was lonely, missing

Pa's long talks and Ma's visits. Luis was more "no-nonsense," checking the firebox, carrying ashes, and filling the reservoir, all as needed, but never visiting.

Luis walked down to the supply store, where Cas was admiring a new flyer.

"Luis, my friend, how are things with you?"

"Fine, Cas. Anything interesting?"

"Yes, there is. This flyer shows the latest invention, available now. You put this gadget in your house, then run a pipe to a tank outside. You run another pipe from the tank to a ditch. Water goes here. You do your private business on this part. They call it a toilet."

Luis studied the picture. "I think my Emma would like this for Christmas. Get me one. I can enclose part of the porch, add a radiator, and make a little room for it. Will that work?"

"Oh, no doubt. I'll start an order and include a radiator."

Luis went home and started enclosing the porch next to the laundry room. He also had an idea about the laundry room, taking the opportunity to add a drain pipe for the wash tub. He and Wolf dug the hole for the outside tank and the overflow trench.

Two weeks later, Cas pulled up in the wagon. "Here it is. Let's set it in place. You pour water here, and then, after you finish, you pull this chain. Look, everything goes away!"

Luis looked at the tank. "It looks difficult to get water into the tank, up near the ceiling like that. Not sure my little ones can manage."

Cas pulled on his mustache. "We could install a pump if you wanted to."

Luis shook his head. "I don't see how they could make that work. Let's think about it, okay?"

Later, Herman got off the train and walked to the old homestead. He was now a state representative and doing very well. His heart jumped, and memories flooded his mind as he watched the dark smoke rising from the chimney and smelled burning wood. Herman walked faster as he got closer until the barn dog announced his arrival with loud, insistent barks.

Herman found Luis working in the barn. "Hey, Luis! How are you doing? I wish I could get back more often, but getting away is hard."

Luis paused, squinting into the bright sunlight from the open door, taking several seconds to recognize his brother. "Quiet, dog.

"Herman, look at you! I am so glad to see you. Glad you could come by. I finished my chores, and now we can visit inside. Emma will be glad you're here. My twin boys are growing faster than spring weeds. And Edith, her family has done well since you left. You won't recognize her children.' Mae is also doing well. Do you remember how you used to torment her? How long can you stay?"

"Only for a couple of days since I'm campaigning a circuit through my district. I'm working the whole trip. But I wanted to see my family. Do you remember how Pa used to talk to the old furnace? He never knew we heard him all over the house, especially after his hearing failed. He told all his secrets to it and consequently to the rest of us."

The two men walked to the house. "Have you married, Herman?"

"No, I haven't. Ma spoiled me. I want a wife as good as her, and they don't exist."

"Well, maybe she was that way because Pa changed. I remember how he was before our little sister died, which wasn't pleasant. Talk about stern! There's no doubt he became a Christian. He was baptized, went to church nearly every week, and listened when we read the Bible. He was still stern, but afterward, he had a different focus. It was as if he had stopped being so selfish or something. I think his conversion was real, not doing it for Ma or anyone else, but because God changed him."

"You are so right, Luis. Whatever Jesus did, we came out ahead."

Cas heard Herman had arrived and came to visit with his old pals. Luis' twins ran to Edith's and Mae's homes to tell them Herman had come.

"Herman, please stay for supper," Emma begged.

After they ate, the three friends visited. They caught up on all the news about each other until near bedtime. The furnace eagerly eavesdropped through the radiators, enjoying their company.

"Luis, I have an idea—your toilet's uptown. Most legislators still have outhouses, even in their city homes. But your point about how hard it is to fill the water tank makes me think. You could run a pipe from the windmill to the tank. Once the tank's full, an overflow could carry the excess to the soil pipe."

"That is a great idea. I think I will see if I can make that work. It will be easy to control the water flow and save a lot of work."

The men began reminiscing.

"Do you remember our house in the old country?" Luis started.

"Yes, I do. It was terrible. But Pa was so proud of that fireplace and chimney. You would have thought he invented the concept, the way he talked about it. Mae and Edith were so small, yet they also had to work hard."

"Yes, it took all of us. That fireplace was our life. It kept us warm, cooked our meals, and kept us busy. Cutting wood was a never-ending chore. Our furnace is a real luxury. Our lives still revolve around feeding it, but we now have much more time for other things." Luis smiled as he remembered.

"We had to do everything the hard way In the Old Country. No matter how hard we worked, we never had anything, and what we had, the Barron took. I have learned about freedom's advantages. It is an important part of what I do in the legislature."

"Remember our wolf hats? They were so warm. We went barefoot when it was warm and wore those awful bark and rag shoes when it was cold. Our thin, tattered coats did so little to keep us warm. I guess the Barron took the best, and we got leftovers."

"It's different here. We keep most of our crops for ourselves and have nice things. Pa changed so much after installing this furnace. The children still go barefoot in the summer, but we have decent boots when it gets cold. I am amazed what a difference a good pair of footwear makes."

The furnace, listening through the radiator, glowed with pride.

Herman chuckled, "Remember when you started mechanizing? It amazed me the last time I was here. That corn shocker's something else. The horse pulls the machine that cuts the corn, and then we tie the bundles. The wheels power the cutter, and the stalks fall into place. We follow later to stand the bundles into shocks. What a time and effort saver."

Luis smiled. "How about when the thresher started coming to town? He set his equipment up, and we threw the sheaves of wheat or oats into its mouth, and it magically separated the grain from the straw. The grain automatically loads onto our wagons. We threw the straw on another wagon for cattle bedding. Everyone in the neighborhood helped, and it became a giant party. Remember when we started roasting a hog for threshing? I think that was Pa's idea, and it became the thing to do. That steam engine belched so much black smoke. How about when it threw sparks into the straw and set it on fire? Talk about making everyone scramble. We were like ants trying to put it out.

"We all worked hard but had a good time. As hard as it was, it was still easier than when we had to do it all by hand."

Cas chuckled at his friends. "I think someday they'll make a machine that, without horses, will run around the fields and gather the crop, separate the straw from the grain, put the kernels into a tank for unloading into a massive wagon. It'll be able to harvest twenty or thirty acres in one day, maybe more."

"You are so dreaming." The others mocked. "What'll power that thing?"

Cas only smiled good-naturedly.

After the laughter died, Luis and Herman discussed other inventions that improved farm life. They nostalgically remembered tools and dogs, the different draft horses, but most fondly, Mae's love of chickens.

The furnace became pensive. *My family has replaced almost everything except me. I am old, have many problems, and need lots of fuel. They work hard, cutting wood and carrying ashes. How long will it be before they replace me, and what will take my place?*

Herman grew quiet, "The worst prank I ever pulled was when I teased Mae about a Ghost Chicken. I feel terrible about that. Did she ever get over it?"

George relayed the story of Hosnick and how Pa solved the gossip problem. He also talked about Pa's church vigil and how he prayed for Mae, setting her free from the nightmares. The men were silent, contemplating the story, when Cas commented, "I never heard the whole story. Now, it all makes sense. I am so glad your father rid the village of Hosnick. What a *pest*."

Now, George bragged about the machine that tied the wheat straw or alfalfa into bales, which were much easier to handle. They loaded them on the wagons before throwing them into the mow. They no longer needed the complicated, time-consuming pully arrangement, which always needed repairs. It took much less labor as well. Herman only shook his head. Cas and George began competing, telling of the changes in the little village.

"You remember when we got the railroad? It brought the world to us, and we made more money for our crops."

"Yep, how about our policeman?"

"Him? Not sure he does anything."

"Ha! And when they made our road gravel instead of rotting logs. Travel became easier."

"Yes, but we still call it our Corduroy Road. I forget what its real name is."

"We have a school teacher now, so the preacher doesn't have to do it."

"How about the flour mill? Not having to grind our grain by hand made everyone happy."

"The blacksmith was great. That man can make or repair anything."

Maybe the blacksmith can fix what's wrong with me? The furnace wondered.

"After all the changes, one wonders what's left to be invented."

The rest of Herman's visit was too short, as he spent time with Mae and Edith, the mayor, the preacher, Cas, and other notable townspeople.

"Why don't you talk to everyone tonight in the church?" The preacher suggested. "You can't possibly visit with everyone; this way, everybody can hear you before you leave tomorrow."

Tomorrow came all too soon. The whole town came to wave goodbye as Herman boarded the train. Then, the farmers returned to their work.

The year was another good one. Luis installed the water line exactly as Herman suggested, except he ran it from the indoor pump. This arrangement worked wonderfully. His wife thought it was his idea. He only told her, "Don't tell anyone; we don't brag."

Fall came, and it was time to wake the furnace, although it was aware of everything anyway. Luis built the first fire, ensuring it burned well, before returning upstairs.

"Luis, did you fire the furnace?" His wife's voice had an edge of annoyance.

"Yes, Emma, I did. Why?"

"It's still cold in here. You think it went out?"

"I'll check." Luis touched the slightly warm radiators before tromping back to the furnace room and opening the firebox, only to see an earthly vision of the fiery pit. "What? I'll throw a little more in, just to be sure."

He bled the air from all the radiators, but it still didn't heat properly. The furnace vainly tried doing better. Luis stacked several straw bales around the foundation to block the wind. Still, the house was not as warm as he wanted. They must manage for a little while.

The next day, he stopped in to see Cas. "It seems my furnace doesn't do the job it used to do. Do you have any ideas?"

Cas scratched his head, then asked, "Have you blown out the accumulated sludge?"

"Huh? I didn't know I was supposed to."

"Why don't you try blowing it all out in the bottom? Refill the water, then blow it out again. Keep doing it until the water's clear. I have a chemical you could put in it that might remove some deposits. Try it and let me know how things are."

Luis went home and did as directed, using a short hose to run the blowdown into buckets. At first, the blowdown was rusty and muddy before becoming clear. Next, he added the chemical. He could hear it gurgling in the pipes, and then he blew it down several times. It seemed the radiators felt warmer after Luis' efforts.

"Ah, Mr. Furnace, we're making progress." The furnace agreed but still felt old and tired.

The next day, Luis talked again with Cas. "That helped. It took all day, but it's better. It's still not right, but it's better. Any other ideas?"

"Well, we can insulate the walls. It helps hold heat in. We pry the top clapboard off, add the insulation, and then put the siding back. We'll also put it in the attic."

Luis stood, watching neighbors walk down the street. "Okay, order the materials."

The insulation helped the tired furnace to do its job. It wasn't like new, but now it was good enough. It needed more fuel, making the chimney smoke blacker and never heating the house properly.

Luis carefully cleaned the chimney every other month during the winter.

Luis continued modernizing his farm over the next few years. He bought a tractor and mechanical shockers that also tied the bundles. Improved plows, planters, and other implements began gracing his barns.

"Emma, I think I want to make a major change." Luis was struggling.

"What's that, dear?"

"I think I want to buy another tractor. This one has worked so well. I want a bigger one that can do more work faster, especially the heavy plowing. And, well, the hard part, I think I should get rid of the draft horses."

"Why?"

Luis took a step backward and stared at the barn. "They eat all the time. Over half our acreage grows food to feed the horses. They still eat whether they're doing something for us or not. I waste time cleaning their stalls, brushing them, and worrying about them. They're getting older, and we must soon replace them regardless."

"You know anything you decide is okay with me."

"I know. But I am trying to do the right thing and need your help deciding."

"Well, that grey one became ornery. We must be careful not to get kicked around it."

"He definitely is ornery, and it is getting worse."

"How'll you get your grain to market, Luis?"

"Well, the railroad spur is not far. I could use the tractor to pull a wagon."

"How about us? How'll we get around?"

"Like now, Emma. Let's keep the carriage horse. He easily handles the road, especially now that it's gravel."

He is getting rid of his horses because they eat too much. I eat a lot. Will he get rid of me as well? The furnace worried more and more.

Now, the pace of change increased. Luis heard about a generator powering an automatic milking machine. This machine allowed him to milk three cows and tend to his other chores until the machines finished. The machine pumped milk into a nearby small tank, bypassing his pails. He always grumbled about cleaning the machine and piping, but overall, he was satisfied.

Then, one day, while buying supplies, Cas broke exciting news. "I heard they're bringing electricity to our little town. They'll run the wires next to the railroad tracks and branch to each home. You might get electrified since your place is on the edge of town."

Luis paused, thought about it for a minute, then nodded.

It took a year, but electricity did come. Everyone wanted it despite the expense. Luis immediately connected his milking machine and installed lights in his house. Leaving the lights on gave him one more thing to fuss at his family about, especially when the bill came.

By now, they had harvested the farm's wooded areas to feed the furnace and progressively dug up the stumps to convert the land to crops. A few small trees on the far side remained, along with trees growing in fence rows. It was nearly Christmas when Luis came in from cutting wood, lugging an armload for the wood box. Emma was busy with her stove, which wouldn't stay lit.

Luis dumped the wood into the box before checking on the furnace. It was okay, with a good fire. The water temperature was nearly perfect, but Luis needed to think. The shadows from the fire danced on the walls. The room was much brighter since Luis installed the electric light bulb.

"Well, Mr. Furnace, Emma looked pretty miserable over that stove. She does a good job, considering how hard it is to cook with. I hate to see her like that. She deserves better. She never complains, but she must be muttering under her breath. Do you have any ideas, Mr. Furnace?"

A log rolled to one side as if on cue, sending sparks up the chimney and causing the fire to burn more brightly. The furnace was happy when Luis visited and wished to be encouraging but was sad as the stove was the same age as it was.

"You're right, Mr. Furnace. I can do something about it, and I will. I remember Pa's stubbornness, and I don't want to be like that."

The next day, Luis met Cas as he opened. "Morning, neighbor. Do you have any stoves in your catalog?"

Cas smiled, "Does your missus know you're here?"

"No. I want to surprise her."

"Well, here's a modern stove. It has four burners and an oven. Best of all, it uses coal oil, which I get in five-gallon cans. Let's see; I can get one in about two weeks if you want it. That will be in time for Christmas."

"Looks good. Order one."

"Okay, will do."

Later that day, Emma walked into the supply store. "Hello, Cas."

"Good morning, Mrs. Schumerhass. What can I do for you?"

"Well, I have a problem. Luis is such a good man and works so hard. He's always cutting wood for the house, and it's hard work. The rest of us help as much as possible, but Luis still does the most. He never complains, starts working before the sun's up, and doesn't finish until after dark. I want to make his work easier. Do you have anything that'll help him?"

Cas sat back on his stool with his thumbs in his suspenders. "Well, there might be. Let's look in our catalog." They thumbed through the catalog.

"Well, look at this. I never noticed it before. This company put a little gasoline motor on a cutting chain. This ad claims it cuts trees like butter. Think it might be what you're looking for?"

Emma studied the advertisement. "Yes, it might be." Then she noticed the price, and her face fell. "I don't have that much money." Her voice got quieter with each word. Cas thought she might cry.

"I'll make a deal with you. Bring me eggs and a few chickens for my table, and I'll give you the saw." They finalized the arrangement, and Emma left, glowing with happiness.

Luis saw her enter the house. "Emma, what happened to you?"

"Oh, nothing. Nothing at all. Everything is fine, more than fine." Emma cheerfully evaded his question.

Luis only shook his head as he put his coat on, silently thinking, *I will never, in my life, understand women.*

Luis and Emma enjoyed their respective Christmas presents. They sometimes opened the windows to keep the stove's smell out of the house. The old wood stove had filled the house with a different scent, more of a sweet forest odor. Burning coal oil reminded the family of a steam engine or factory. Regardless, Emma thought that the stench was a small price to pay for the stove's convenience and was exceptionally happy with it.

Luis bought forty acres of wooded land close to his homestead. Now, he had enough trees to heat his house for a long time and a chainsaw to cut them. These trees were mainly hardwood but not as big as the ones they had, but they would make good fuel. The soil was rocky and not suitable for crops.

Soon, Luis converted the inside water pump to an electrically driven one. Luis still used the windmill for his cattle, insisting electricity was too expensive. Steadily, he continued upgrading his farm equipment. Farming was still hard work, but mechanization enabled Luis to continue farming. Wolf feared the new, fancy equipment and would only do hand work. He liked cutting wood by himself during the winter, using the cross-cut saw. He always disappeared when Luis started a tractor or the chainsaw, reappearing a few minutes after the engines stopped.

All of Luis' sons except his twins, George and Otto, moved to the big city, and now only the four lived in the giant house. "Emma, this is almost like when we first arrived. Imagine Oscar living by himself in this lonely house. Our youngest ones have ventured into the world, and now we're left here."

"Ah, but we have family nearby. Edith's down the road, as are her children and their children. Mae lives across town, and her children are grown up as well. We see them all the time. I'm sad because my family has passed, but I love my in-laws, nephews, and nieces. Oscar had no one, which is why I think he adopted you and your family." Emma smiled as she thought about their extended family.

Luis felt the radiator. "This doesn't have the heat it should," Luis disappeared towards the furnace room.

II

WOLF

"WOLF, HOW ABOUT STARTING CHORES WHILE I GET MORE COAL? YOU can help me unload when I get back. It's still cold enough that we might need the heat. I'll get some for you as well." Luis started the day's work.

"Sir, do I have to use the milking machine?" Wolf hated automation.

Luis thought momentarily, "It won't hurt you, Wolf. You know how; why don't you want to use it?"

"I don't know. It makes these funny noises. It might be alive."

"Now, Wolf, the cows don't mind it. You're smarter than them; you shouldn't mind it either."

"What if something happens? What if it hurts a cow? What should I do?" Wolf's hands trembled uncontrollably, and he kept wiping his forehead as he glanced at the road.

"It's okay, Wolf; you don't have to do the milking. Tell you what, you feed the animals while I do the milking, and then we can get the coal together. Is that all right with you?"

"Thank you, Mr. Luis. Thank you very much." Wolf relaxed and immediately ran toward the barn.

Wolf climbed into the mow to get feed while Luis milked the cows. Luis filled several cans with milk from the storage tank. Both men carried the milk to the creamer in the basement. Wolf turned the creamer's handle while Luis poured the milk into the creamer, setting some aside for his family. "Wolf, you want any milk?"

"No, sir. I don't need any. Thank you, though." Wolf was always respectful, to the point of annoyance. Luis didn't dare let him know he overdid the formalities.

The cream, once separated, fell with "glopping" noises into the stainless creamer pail. They filled several cans with cream before Wolf started carrying the residual up and out of the basement. He slopped the residual skim milk into the hog troughs, running back to get more loads. The hogs always greedily piled on each other, squealing as they fought to get more than their share.

The furnace listened to the men working and filling the cream cans. Luis filled a smaller jar with cream, which he set aside to cool in the damp basement. The last thing he did before leaving was to call to Emma, "Cream is in the basement, ready to churn as soon as it is cool." They made more butter than they needed but were very generous, giving Mae and Edith as much as they wanted. Ma sold a little to Mabel for her boarding house.

"Okay, Wolf, let's get the coal." Getting more coal made the furnace happy, as he knew Luis would continue feeding him. Luis noticed Wolf's fear as he started the tractor and began the short journey to the supply store.

The two men loaded the coal, and Wolf waited with the wagon while Luis paid. Wolf sat hunched on the wagon seat, his hat pulled tight, almost covering his eyes, his knees pressed tightly together, his hands clutching each other, and neither looking at nor speaking to passersby. Everyone in town knew him by now, and while they thought him strange, the neighbors were always kind to Wolf. Sometimes, when Luis didn't need his help, Wolf wandered to another neighbor to ask for work. No one knew what he did with his money; he didn't waste it on clothes or much else.

Wolf wouldn't go to church with Luis and the family. Yet, they could see him outside a window most Sundays, listening to the service. Luis often heard him softly sing a hymn while working, but only if he thought he was alone. Emma believed that Wolf had such kindness that he had to know Jesus. Emma and Luis constantly wondered what happened to Wolf to make him terrified of people.

Most people treated Wolf fairly, except the village miser, who always took advantage of Wolf. Wolf soon learned to avoid him. Wolf was very respectful to the miser despite being cheated.

They only knew him as Wolf, the name he used when forced to introduce himself. No one thought he looked like a wolf, and they privately wondered why he chose that name. Wolf rapidly became a village legend. No one knew how old he was, but everyone suspected he was in his late fifties or maybe older. Without a past, he became part of ever-increasing wild stories.

Once back at the farm, Wolf immediately began shoveling the coal into the coal bin. Luis watched him work; *He always takes the hardest jobs. One day, as hard as he works, he will work himself to death. I had best not let him catch me watching him. It makes him so nervous, like the time he wet his pants.*

Luis spoke to Wolf, "Hey, Wolf. Do you mind finishing unloading the coal? After you finish, I'll help put the tractor and wagon in the shed. I need to talk with Emma for a minute."

"Yes sir, no problem at all. Thank you, sir."

Luis walked into the house and found his wife busy on her stove. "Emma, it smells like you are making another feast. You want me to invite Wolf for dinner?"

"Will you? It makes him so nervous when I invite him. I worry about him. Do you know what he does in that little house after work?"

"No, I've wondered. I've gone over to talk with Wolf several times, and he is always just sitting in a chair, staring at the wall. I'm not sure he even lights a fire when it's cold. I rarely see any lantern light. I gladly give him fuel. I have seen him washing his clothes occasionally, although he has few. Maybe I could gift him some shirts and pants for Christmas."

Luis watched until Wolf nearly finished unloading the coal before walking outside. "Wolf, Emma made a powerful good meal, and we want to share it with you so that it won't go to waste. How about you do the noon chores while I put the tractor and wagon away? I know how good you are with the animals, and it seems they like you better than me."

Wolf was embarrassed. "No sir, they like you fine."

"Ah, no. But, you make the cows happy, and a happy cow makes more milk, at least that's what my Pa used to say."

Wolf proudly walked to the barn to throw alfalfa in the cow's manger. "Hello, Mrs. Cow. How are you today? You are looking fine."

Wolf patted each cow's forehead and talked to each one, always calling them Mrs. Cow, no matter what anyone else called them. They always looked back at him, following him with their gaze while they chewed. Once, Luis tried convincing himself that the cows didn't smile when Wolf entered the barn.

It was almost noon when the two men walked into the house to wash up. George and Otto, now nearly grown, spent the morning working on pasture fences and were already seated at the table. Wolf waited until Luis finished washing his hands. Emma, always the observant one, noted every detail. Wolf wouldn't sit until after Luis sat. As they pulled their chairs to the table, Emma placed stew, biscuits, and a mug of strong coffee in front of each.

"Emma, I like these meals. They remind me so much of Ma and the old country, not that the old country is worth remembering. Ma used to cook like this for special occasions. Otherwise, we had parched corn. Although it wasn't half as good as yours, she could cook a good stew." Emma smiled at her husband's affectionate praise.

Emma served a still-warm cherry pie as soon as they finished the stew.

George started talking about the afternoon's chores. "I think the far side of the barn needs repairs. It looks like a cow kicked a few boards loose. Unless you have something else for Otto and me, how about we fix it? We'll have to move manure, and who knows what to get to it, so it'll take some time. We better knock this job out before farming gets serious."

Luis turned to his hired man, "Wolf, would you help these two? I think they need your guidance." All three put their coats on and walked out.

Immediately after they left, Emma chastised Luis, "Luis, don't do that to him. You know how it upsets him and makes him so nervous. Did you see how he reacted? I thought he might throw up. He thinks of your sons like they are you. He wouldn't dare try to show them something. Who knows how he will take your flippancy?"

"Now, Emma, I didn't mean anything. I was teasing George and Otto, not Wolf." Luis was suitably contrite.

"Well, Luis, He is so uncomfortable around us. I think he only eats with us because you ask him. I think he would rather eat with the cows."

"Wolf certainly relates to animals better than people."

"That's right. Do you notice that Wolf does exactly what you do? Today, for example, you wet your left hand and then reached for the soap. You lathered, rinsed, and used the rag to wash your face. He did what you did in the same order. Then, he waited until you sat down. You ate some stew, a bite of biscuit, and sipped a little coffee. He took the same number of bites of stew, a bite of biscuit, followed by a sip of coffee. You put your elbows on the table while waiting for the pie, and he did as well. You finished your coffee while leaning back in your chair, and he leaned back exactly as you did."

Luis was confused, "Emma, how long have you noticed this?"

"Since he ate with us the first time. He doesn't know how to act, so he acts like you. I don't think it's a problem, but you must know what he is doing. He looks up to you in a most powerful way."

Luis furrowed his brow, "Do you feel safe around him? If you don't, I'll run him off before you can say lickety-split."

Emma laughed, "I feel very safe around him. I think he's like a watchdog. I believe he'd give his life to protect the farm and especially your family if anything threatened us. He knows how precious we are to you."

"Okay, what do you suggest we do to make him more comfortable?"

"I don't know, but I do know pushing him makes him uncomfortable."

"Well, I best be getting my work done." With that, Luis left the house and headed toward the barn. *I need to check on those two rascals and be sure they aren't throwing manure at each other or whatever else they can think of to get into trouble—hard telling.*

George looked up as soon as Luis turned the corner. "Hi, Father. Have you seen Wolf? He left the house after lunch but never showed up back here."

Luis turned and walked to Wolf's house. He knocked, didn't hear anyone, and entered, "Wolf, you okay?" But the little house was empty. Luis looked around and saw everything was in order; Wolf had neatly tucked the bed's covers under the mattress. The old kerosene lamp quietly sat on the tiny table with the single chair. Everything was so perfect that it seemed out of the ordinary.

Luis walked to the road and, squinting, saw someone looking like Wolf walking away from town in the distance. He had an unusual gait:

his left leg took longer steps than his right, and he always turned a little to the right, making it look like he walked sideways with a limp. It was Wolf. Luis went back into the house and found Emma.

"Emma, I think Wolf left again."

"Do you think he will be all right? I hope he doesn't die of exposure in this weather."

"I don't know, but he does this every so often. Do you think it is because I said something about the boys needing his guidance? I feel terrible about it."

"No, Luis, I don't think so. We don't know what goes on in his mind. He's definitely in a different place mentally."

"I'm going let him go, like all the other times, and we will see if he returns. If he does, we won't say a word." Luis went to the barn and told his sons about Wolf.

The weather started warming, and Luis considered what to plant in each field. "I wish Wolf was back. His labor made so much go easier, especially for the crops planted furthest from the barn." He complained to his wife.

One Sunday, Luis entered the barn to feed the cows the noon alfalfa, when as he approached the manger, a dusty cloud of feed fell from the mow. Looking up, he saw Wolf, horrified he had almost buried his boss.

"Hello, Wolf. I see you're already feeding the cows. How do they look to you?"

"Mr., Mr. Luis, they're looking good. I'm almost done and will be down in a minute." Another cloud descended into the manger, followed by the hired man, although he used the ladder.

"Careful, Wolf, we need you without broken bones."

"Yes, sir, Mr. Luis. What do you want me to do next?"

George and Otto showed up, and Luis decided to take the afternoon off. Wolf immediately headed to his little house. Otto dared his brother, "Do you think you could get us a couple of squirrels for supper before I do?" with that, they raced to get their guns and headed toward the woodlot. Luis decided a nap was his priority.

Spring came and brought the hard work of tilling and planting. Luis and his sons drove the equipment while Wolf carried seed bags, fed the livestock, and stayed out of the way.

Once the crops emerged, daylight usually found Wolf hoeing weeds. Luis told him to eat with them, and Wolf always mimicked him. As soon as they finished their meal, Wolf always rose to feed the cattle before returning to his field.

"Emma, Wolf must hate weeds. He is out there at dawn and works until dark. I think we have the cleanest fields in the state. The corn won't have much competition from weeds, and we'll get a bigger crop because of Wolf's work." Luis was proud of Wolf.

That Summer, Wolf left twice for a couple of days. No one knew where he went or what he did, and Wolf never said. Luis asked him once, and all Wolf did was make a little grunting sound and look at his feet.

The furnace heard the parents talking in late fall after everyone went to bed. "Another thing, Emma, I think our hired man, Wolf, finally left for good. I went by his little house, which was neat and clean, just like always, but he was nowhere to be found. The day before he left, I found him staring at a tractor, with his hand on a tire, muttering something about missing horses."

Emma voiced her concern. "I thought he might leave soon. He's wandered off before but always came back. People like him can't seem to stay in one place for long. He has never been gone this long before. I think the tractors make him nervous; maybe he thinks life is passing him by."

Luis responded, "You're right. He relates to animals better than people and struggles with machines. Well, our boys are grown. We can manage without him, especially since we started using our tractors. They surely make life easier. Despite his strange ways, I'll miss Wolf. We should keep his little house as it is in case he comes back."

"Luis, it bothers me. What happened to him? Did we do something to offend him?"

Luis was very uneasy. "Emma, I don't know. We did all we could to make him feel comfortable, maybe even too much. But, if you hadn't fed him, I'm not sure what he would have eaten. I never saw him get any food or anything. Where did he get his clothes? I never saw him spend his pay. He has been here for quite a while, and, sorry to say, I don't know if he was contented or not or if he had family somewhere. Maybe I pushed him too hard to use the new equipment.

"He just wouldn't talk about himself. He only replied to my questions with grunts. We need to try harder to reach him if he comes back. Who knows how he thinks and interprets what others say or do."

Luis briefly thought before continuing, "I wonder if our family's closeness bothered Wolf. We are so blessed. I am continually amazed at how well our boys get along, even when they must do the worst jobs. They continually joke between themselves, laugh, and make a game out of everything. I never saw them show Wolf anything except kindness or say anything that was even slightly mean. Those two kids are exceptional. After doing the smallest favor, they reward each other with a sincere 'thank you.' What a blessing."

"Yes, they do get along. They hardly get angry at each other, and when they do, they don't seem to be able to stay mad for more than a few minutes."

Luis was ready to sleep. Even the furnace was getting tired of all the talking. "I don't know, Emma, I don't know. I don't understand Wolf and probably never will. But I have a big day tomorrow. Good night."

The furnace thought about Wolf leaving and worried if farm life was passing it by as well.

12

The War

Luis sat at Sunday dinner, thinking about the past year. He knew the farm did well due to his family's hard work. High prices for his crops helped, and his livestock did better. He hadn't lost any calves to sickness; all his poultry laid more eggs than he could use or sell, every sow had litters of 12 or more piglets, and grain and alfalfa overflowed his barns. *Prosperity is the best problem,* but *what should I do with my bounty? Maybe I should buy another forty acres. Well, it's time to get to work.*

Luis cleared his throat. "George and Otto, will you do the noon chores today? Thanks." The two young men went to the barn. By now, they understood this meant their parents wanted to discuss something without them. The furnace listened carefully through the radiators.

"Luis, did you notice our sons were sitting on either side of that Hammersmech girl in church this morning? I think they're sweet on her. What's her first name?" Emma's concern caused her voice to waver slightly.

Luis chose his words carefully. "I noticed. She's pretty, but I don't know much about her family. They usually attend church."

Emma fretted, wringing her hands in that slight way concerned mothers have. "Yes, she's pretty. Portcia, that's her name. I don't know much about her or her family either. But both boys can't have her. That family recently moved here, and Mrs. Hammersmech usually joins the ladies' group. Yet, she is hard to get to know, doesn't talk much about her family or background."

"I know nothing about her husband, only that he leaves quickly after church and farms on the South side of town. What should we do? If I talk to our boys, I fear they'll start sneaking around our backs." Like the typical male, Luis wanted to barge in, take action, and solve the problem.

"Oh yes, Luis, you're right. I don't know what we should do either. Maybe keep an eye on them." Emma focused on family harmony. The two balanced each other very well. The furnace briefly burned intently as it listened to this exchange.

Sunday was a welcome rest day when they only did minimum work. They fed livestock, tended to the furnace, cooked, and such. After that, the family sat in the sitting room until supper and talked. The two boys, uncharacteristically, were quiet. At the same time, Luis and Emma chatted about the weather, the chickens, the neighbor's dog, and all the other topics of farm life. During supper, the two boys ate in silence, never looking up. The stilted conversation betrayed everyone, who had the same thing on their minds. Twice, Luis cleared his throat but then thought better of it and went back to his potatoes.

"Hey guys, time to get the evening milking done." Luis thought the boys working together might thaw their emotions a little. "Tell you what, you two do the milking, and I'll feed the cattle." It was an order, not a question.

The two boys trudged to the barn, followed by their father. Luis climbed into the mow for hay while the boys set up the milking machine. It wasn't two minutes before he heard the commotion, with them calling each other names and threatening significant bodily harm.

"Hey, what in the world is going on?" Luis stepped between them and held both boys apart, one in each of his mighty hands.

George, always the leader, started, "It's nothing. My obnoxious brother must learn to do his work and not depend on others."

Otto sputtered, "What kind of lies are you spreading? I carry my share around here. You can't even get out of bed in the morning."

Then they both began accusing each other of every known sin, neither listening to what the other was saying, both shouting at the same time and trying to be the loudest.

"Enough!" Luis roared. "You two settle down right now. This fight is terrible. Apologize! And make it sincere."

"I'm sorry," George began, then paused.

"I'm sorry you're such a liar," replied Otto.

They both struggled, swinging their fists. Luis, even with his oversized build, barely restrained them. The twins were careful not to hit their father, rightly fearing the consequences.

"Stop it! Now! Listen to me. I am ashamed of both of you. I will release you, and I want you both to go to your rooms and not say another word. Not one word; do you understand me? I'll finish here." Both barely nodded.

Luis carefully released the rebels, and they quietly slunk into the house while Luis finished the chores. Once inside, he only shook his head at his wife.

Emma began, "I could hear the commotion all the way here. Now what?"

"I don't know. Our boys used to get along so. What happened?"

The furnace heard the two young men stomping around in their rooms. George clumped from his door to his window, where he paused and stared at the barn before marching back to the door. Otto merely paced, his heavy boots echoing in the room below.

Emma looked at George, "My, but they're restless."

Luis, in a dull, tired way, spoke up. "I think it's that Hammersmech girl. This mess started as soon as we got back from church. As you know, no other single women their age live in our little village."

"I think you're right. It looks like Portcia is playing our boys against each other. Maybe she doesn't have such a good head after all."

"I wonder if we should send one of them to live with Herman for a few months." Luis picked at his fingernails, trying to distract himself.

Emma pressed forward, "How would you choose? Both will assume you think the girl should be the other's."

"I hate these problems. Crops fail, cows die, but this is harder to know what to do."

Emma hugged her husband. "You think I should talk to her mother? Would that help?"

Luis stared at his wife. *What did I do to deserve someone who always wades into the most difficult problems, trying to improve them?* "I don't know; why don't you try if you think it'll help."

The furnace heard it all and knew the only thing it could do was keep the family warm. *I wish I could do something,* it thought.

The family ate breakfast in silence the next day. After they finished, Luis gave the day's marching orders. "Otto, you get more coal, and George, hitch the horse to the carriage before doing chores."

Neither son liked the back-breaking work of getting coal. They must shovel it into the wagon and then unload it into the coal bin. It was strenuous work and easier when two men worked together. One moved coal to the back of the wagon, and the other shoveled it into the coal bin. Two men working together avoided a lot of walking, especially when they unloaded the wagon's front end. Otto resented getting the worst assignment but was glad not to work with his brother.

Chores included milking cows, collecting eggs, and feeding livestock. George particularly despised cleaning the milking equipment. It was a never-ending task that grated on him and his lack of patience. His father always checked his work and made him redo it if it wasn't good enough. But two men working together handled the awkward equipment more easily. George resented getting the worst assignment but was glad not to work with his brother.

Both sons grumbled under their breath on their way out.

Luis lost his temper. "That's enough! I don't know what's happening, but we don't like it and won't have it! Do you two understand me?"

George and Otto silently turned and quietly seethed as they left for their assignments.

"I thought dividing the chores would help them understand how much easier life is if they work together. It doesn't look like it will help. I'll take you to town," Luis told his wife. "I want to talk with the preacher."

When they returned, Luis told George to put the horse up. Otto had lackadaisically started unloading the coal, which angered George that he had to do more work while his brother was wasting time.

Inside, Emma started. "That was a failure. I talked with her, and she doesn't see anything wrong with what her girl does. She commented, '

You're only young once; her girl should have fun while she can.' Should I talk with the girl? Maybe she should make it clear which boy, if either, she prefers?"

Luis groaned. "The preacher said he'll talk to both but told me to expect it wouldn't do much good. He has seen this problem before. It ended up with one son killing the other and then receiving a life sentence. Don't waste your time talking with the girl."

Luis's speech saddened the furnace.

George came into the dining room. Luis stopped him before he hung his coat up and told him to follow. Freshly fallen snow had turned everything a beautiful white, unspoiled in its beauty. The white powder muffled every sound except their heavy boots. There was no wind, and the air hinted at wanting to warm up. The sky had a few high clouds, and the setting sun shone brilliantly against the horizon. *This is the perfect time for a nice quiet walk*, thought Luis. *I wish I could enjoy it more.*

They silently walked until they reached the back forty, where Luis turned and looked George in the eye. "George, I know something serious is going on. I want you to tell me what it is."

George silently looked down at his boots. Luis thought his face got a little redder, although it might have been the cold wind.

"Okay, I'll guess. Your fighting with Otto looks like a girl problem. Is it?"

George snapped to attention, his eyes burning into his father's. "There's this girl I like, Portcia Hammersmech. She said she likes me too. It's getting time for me to start my own family."

Luis opened his mouth, then, thinking better of it, closed it, waiting.

George looked away. "Yesterday, while we were milking, Otto told me he has a girl now. Portcia is his girl! He told me she likes him and he likes her. I called him a liar, and you know how that ended."

Luis nodded. "George, I want to ask you a favor. I'm not telling you what to do; I'm only asking for a favor. Will you talk with the preacher about this girl? And while you're at it, stop fussing with your brother."

George looked down and shuffled his feet slightly. "Yes, Father, I'll talk with the preacher."

"Son, let's go back to the house. I know this is hard, but you'll figure it out. Maybe you should stay away from Otto for a while." Luis gently slapped George's back while George nodded.

Once back at the house, Luis found Otto. "Get your coat; we need to walk."

The two men walked silently to the back forty, with their hands in their coat pockets, following the snow prints George and Luis had made earlier.

Otto looked at his father, "I know why you brought both of us here."

"So, tell me your side."

"While we were milking, George told me how much he likes Portcia Hammersmech and how much she likes him. I couldn't believe such lies and didn't know who had started what. I only remember how angry I got, and he was also angry. After all, she's my girl, and he can't steal her! Something rose within me, and I needed him to take it back."

"Otto, I want to ask you the same favor I asked your brother. Will you talk with the preacher about Portcia? I think he has good advice. Also, please stop fussing with George."

Reluctantly, even hesitantly, Otto barely answered, "I'll talk with him."

The two men silently walked back, Otto giving no sign of what he was thinking, while Luis could only pray. They could see winter storm clouds gathering on the horizon, chasing away the hints of warmer weather. The tormented sky would bring a new layer of snow later that night, returning the farm to pristine beauty. They reached the farmhouse after dark.

That night, the furnace overheard Luis talking with Emma. "I don't know what to do. It's about the Hammersmech girl. They both agreed to talk with the preacher. Neither agreed to stop fighting with the other."

Both downcast sons returned from their counseling. George wordlessly ate supper, his mind somewhere else. Otto talked incessantly about everything except women. As soon as supper was over, the furnace heard them both clump to their rooms, where they went to bed.

Luis looked at Emma, "Well, what do you think?"

"I don't know. Maybe we should send both to live with Herman for a while. I don't like the way this looks at all. Neither boy was their usual self at supper, and this situation will only lead to more problems. I hope the preacher's wrong about killing each other, but they're surely angry enough. I think they could do it; maybe both kill the other. What a mess."

For the rest of the week, Luis was careful to do what he could to keep the young men apart. They were civil to each other, hardly saying anything unnecessary. Several times, Luis noticed their tempers were close to flaring and intervened by giving one something to do elsewhere. Both boys avoided looking at each other or their father.

Sunday rolled around, and the two men sat on either side of Portcia in church again.

At dinner, Luis addressed his sons. "I think you two are grown enough and should start sitting on the men's side of the church."

Both sons silently fumed, knowing disobedience was not an option.

The following week was uneventful. Whatever truce existed maintained peace, at least on the surface.

Sunday, after they finished dinner and the noon chores, George quietly stepped out of the house. Otto saw him walking toward town and stealthily followed him. George stopped at the Hammersmech house, knocked on the door, and Portcia answered and let him in. Otto stood on the road, watching and stewing in the cold wind.

As soon as George stepped from the house, Otto confronted him.

"What're you doing here, George?"

"You need to mind your own business!"

The town policeman knocked on Luis' door just before supper. "Luis, I have some bad news for you. I had to arrest your sons for publicly fighting this afternoon."

"What? Come in, Norris, and tell me what happened! Sit down for a minute."

The policeman was uncomfortable and kept squirming. "It seems that one went calling on the Hammersmech girl. The other waited for him, and when he came out, somehow, they got into a fight. No one knows what happened, and they aren't talking. When I got there, I needed help pulling them off each other. They banged themselves up badly, but I think it's mostly bruising. I thought it best to lock them up overnight to help them cool off. I'm sorry."

Emma could only lightly cover her mouth. Luis slumped in his chair, putting his head into his hands. Finally, he looked up, shook his head, and spoke to his wife. "We forget our manners. Get Norris some coffee," and then to the officer, "Thank you for telling us."

As all good friends do, Norris sat silently with the grieving parents until they finished their coffee before leaving.

The next day, Luis went to the village jail for his sons. The village had a lot of controversy about building two cells since they had never needed even one before. Still, since they were growing, most citizens agreed with the plan. Norris had one twin in each cell. Luis could see their anger towards each other as they silently walked home, one on each side of Luis. Both sons sensed Luis' disappointment and shame.

The week crawled by uneventfully until Sunday, during the after-church potluck. Luis and Emma watched their sons as they milled around and visited. That night, the furnace overheard them discussing the day.

"I don't like this at all." Emma started. "Portcia was flirting with both."

"I saw it as well. We can't let this continue, or our boys will kill each other like Cain killed Abel. Portia enjoys tormenting our sons."

Nothing else happened until the following Sunday. After church, Luis saw Portcia tug Otto's sleeve, and the two disappeared behind the building. George followed, as did Luis. Once hidden, Portcia snuggled next to Otto and gave him a short peck on his cheek before bouncing away laughing. George only turned and marched home.

At dinner, Luis started. "Look, men, I have been around for a few years and need to share something. It seems to me that Portcia is playing both of you. She likes the conflict and does her best to stir it up. Think about this. Could you live with someone like that? If you win her, she'll cause nothing but trouble. She also flirts with married men. Do you see how she looks at Fiezer? He has only been married a couple of years, has a wonderful wife and a little boy, and she's making eyes at him?"

Otto jumped, shouting, "I can't take this," before stomping into his room.

George rushed to the barn.

The furnace only knew that emotions were high. Luis opened the firebox and threw in a shovel of coal and some wood before sitting on Pa's old log.

"Pa used to come down here and, somehow, while talking to the furnace, he solved his problems. Okay, Mr. Furnace, what answers do you have?"

The furnace only maintained a steady burn. "You're right, as always, Mr. Furnace. There's nothing more I can do. Sending one or both away will only cause more problems. I'll have to wait to see how this works out. But I can pray. Maybe God will have mercy on us and intervene."

Luis noticed his sons' growing resentment against him for the rest of the winter. Both sullenly did their work and kept conversations to a minimum.

One night, the furnace overheard the parents.

"Luis, it looks like they're avoiding the Hammersmech girl. Do you think they're over her?"

"No, Emma, they're still smitten." Luis sighed sadly. "I don't know what else to do. If this keeps up, we will have a major fight. Worse, I think they're furious with us. Our family used to be so close; now, well, I don't know what to do. She isn't leaving them alone, even if they try to leave her alone. Every Sunday seems slightly worse, with Portcia pouring more fuel on the fire. I can't imagine going to church to flirt, but she's okay with it. Do we need to stop going?"

"You know that won't solve anything, Luis."

"Emma, if the preacher is right and one kills the other, he'll go to jail for the rest of his life or worse. We won't have anyone to take our farm."

"Luis, stop thinking like that and go to sleep. Nothing bad has happened yet, and there is enough time to worry about it after it happens. God will take care of us. He always has and always will. You know our sons are more important to God than even the farm. Now, please, stop fretting about what you can't control and go to sleep."

Both parents laid on their backs and stared at the ceiling, Luis with his arms crossed and Emma with one arm over her eyes. Neither parent rested well, spending most of the night, like every recent night, silently praying and trying their best not to worry. Later, Luis would comment on how hard it was to trust God during his great need. It did something to him, making him call on his Lord quicker.

Spring came, and grudgingly, the sons helped with farm work. After the villagers finished their planting, the neighborhood returned to a slower, friendlier pace as neighbors again had time to visit. Cas kept his coffee pot full, thinking he would sell more the longer his friends stayed. As always, the men argued about imaginary problems, called each other silly names, told terrible jokes, and acted like men usually act.

One day, Luis was a little late to the supply store conversation. "Morning, Cas, neighbors. How're things with you?"

"You hear about that new station master for the railroad? He showed up yesterday and moved into the railroad blockhouse. He seems nice and has a wife, two older daughters, and several younger boys. He said he wanted to stay here and was tired of the big city. They'll be a fine addition to our little community."

Then the conversation drifted to how little the railroad paid for their grain and arguments about why some sows had large litters, and others had small ones. Like always, they solved nothing, but the men enjoyed the debates.

Later that afternoon, Emma went to her church ladies' group, meeting in Edith's home. They stretched the base fabric over the quilting frame for a new quilt, one they would give to the next woman who married. As always, they speculated about who'll get it.

Mabel, the local roadhouse proprietor, already knew. "Ladies, we had a marriage last night." She fluttered her hand before her to be sure she had everyone's attention.

"What! Who?" The women all leaned forward to better concentrate on the news.

Smug with the power of new gossip, Mabel drew it out. "You didn't hear? It was that Hammersmech girl. She linked up with that new guy staying in my roadhouse."

"He just came to town a couple of weeks ago. What's Portcia doing with him?"

Mabel went on, "You know how she is. And he's worse. As I hear it, he's a gambler, running from a murder out East." Facts no longer mattered.

"You don't say!"

"What're they going to do?"

Mabel continued, basking in her glory, "I hear he has lots of money. He told me he was going to Chicago and needed a short rest, so he stayed here. He's a good tenant, pays in cash, walks to the edge of town in the morning, and then returns for dinner. He likes to sit on the porch and watch the world go by for the rest of the day."

"Why would Portcia want him?" Every woman forgot about the quilt while breathlessly waiting for the answer.

Mabel arrogantly sneered, "You ever see how much gold he carries? He always has a pistol near his hand. I would, too, if I carried that much gold." Her tone of voice betrayed how much she despised her tenant.

"I don't think we'll finish this quilt before they need it." Mabel dangled bait for the juiciest part.

"Why do you say that? It won't be cold for a few months, and we have time."

Mabel wickedly laughed the cruel laugh of a gossip, "They left town right after the ceremony. It wasn't even a proper church ceremony; instead, it took place by the new courthouse. He packed his bag, more like a small bundle, and she only had the clothes on her back. I heard him tell her he would buy her everything she needed once they got to Chicago, although I couldn't understand where he put all his gold. Portcia acted like her knight in shining armor carried her off. They left on horseback, not even a proper carriage, if you can imagine. Her mother didn't know anything about it until the so-called wedding. You ask me; I think it was a shotgun wedding. That's probably why Mrs. Hammersmech isn't here. She must be embarrassed, the poor thing."

"Do tell!"

"You don't say."

The comments and attention fed Mabel's ego, her smile betraying her. A tiny voice in her head whispered: "it'll be hard for them to top this." The ladies, however, had begun discussing which pattern to use for the quilt's top.

That night at supper, the furnace heard Luis clear his throat. "Emma, I heard we have a new family in town. I haven't met them yet, but the new stationmaster has arrived. Sounds like a nice family."

"Luis, I also heard some news. Portcia eloped with one of Mabel's roadhouse customers."

Both sons snapped their heads to attention as if shot.

"Don't know much about him, but Mabel claims he is rich."

Both parents skillfully guided the conversation to how the chickens were doing until after supper.

The furnace heard the boys after everyone else went to bed. First, George knocked on Otto's door.

"Otto, I want to apologize."

"George, I was as much wrong as anyone. That girl played us both. Our parents are right."

"Emma, isn't it amazing how this worked out? I never thought the girl would leave the picture, especially like this." Luis smiled in the dark.

"Luis, it's amazing."

"You know, Ma was right. God guided us from the old country to Oscar and now this. He's so good, especially to us. I'm very thankful but don't thank Him nearly enough."

"Yes, God has been good to us. We live in a nice town, which is growing. Our farm and our children are doing well. I hope Mrs. Hammersmech and the girl are all right. I suspect she has chosen a difficult life, much harder than our simple village life."

The furnace settled in for the night. Luis had started a small fire to banish the outside chill. Warm water circulated to the different radiators and back. His fire burned slowly, providing just enough heat. Occasionally, ash fell into the ash bin, glowing a cherry red. The furnace listened to each family member, some breathing softly but none snoring like Luis. *I can always tell how his day went by how loud he is,* the furnace thought. Outside, the wind gently blew. Cattle made their contented mooing sounds, and a dog barked at the moon somewhere. The furnace contentedly did its job.

The crop yields that year were average, but the corn and wheat prices more than made up for it. Luis continued mechanizing the farm, buying new equipment and, his pride and joy, an automobile. He could never bring himself to say "car" or "automobile;" instead, it was always "The Machine." He sold his carriage horse and buggy and continued improving his operation at every chance.

One fall day, Otto approached his father. "May I talk with you?"

"Sure, what's on your mind?"

"I went to the barbershop a few days ago and saw this flyer in the window. It was a recruiting flyer for the army. I've thought about it and think I'd like to join."

Luis paused, "You know we left the old country to avoid the military?"

"Yes, sir. But George wants to farm, and there isn't much else for me here."

"You could farm together."

"We could, but I don't want to farm. You don't need me, anyway, what with all the new machinery. This flyer claims the army wants officers. I'll go to officer school if I pass the testing. It is a six-year commitment, and if it doesn't work out, I'll do something else."

"We're probably going to war in Europe. You might not come back." Concern furrowed Otto's brow.

"Yes, I know that. I heard about the commotion on the barber's radio."

"Well, Otto, I don't like it. But if that's what you want to do, go for it."

"Thanks, Father. By the way, I've already talked to Mother about it."

"Little boy, I should give you a whipping for going behind my back. What did she say?"

Otto smiled at his father's unusual methods of showing affection. "She cried, hugged me, and said, 'Do what you think best.' I'll need to leave next week."

Otto's announcement saddened the furnace. *I wonder if I will ever see him again. I am getting old and worn out, and the military is dangerous. Luis is the only one left. The rest of the family is all new.*

The family stood on the train platform in the warm sun. In the bright, clear sky, several distant eagles drifted on unseen air currents toward the forest. At the last minute, Otto hugged his mother, shook hands with his brother and father, then bravely mounted the train with his sack of clothes and a fresh cherry pie wrapped in a napkin that his mother suddenly thrust into his hands. The train chugged off minutes later, steam and smoke billowing from the engine's exhaust.

Luis turned to Emma, "That train looks mighty big, taking our mighty small son into the mighty cruel world." Emma couldn't answer, only crying while embracing her husband. George looked at his feet and shuffled before turning, his hands in his pockets, and resolutely walked back to the house.

"Let's go, Emma. Our Machine waits."

"Oh, Luis, I forgot to give Otto a fork. How will he eat his pie?" Luis only smiled and took his wife's hand, leading her to The Machine.

13

REPLACED

Now, THE YEARS PASSED QUICKLY. AT FIRST, OTTO WROTE FREQUENTLY, telling them of boot camp and his training. Then, he told them how convinced he was that he had made the right decision and his several promotions. They enjoyed his yearly leave, but, always too soon, it was time for him to leave.

George married one of the stationmaster's girls, Anna, and soon had several children. They moved into Luis' house to care for his aging parents. A letter from Herman's attorney arrived, informing them of Herman's passing. Herman left his estate to several charities.

Luis looked at his wife, "I can't believe Herman is gone. He did well and never married, but he helped our state. We will miss him, for sure."

George and Luis decided to hunt squirrels one crisp winter day. They started at the far end of their land and then gradually went deep into the forest, where many shallow streams were like shallow sloughs. The ground was so rocky no one wanted to buy it from the Federal Government. The villagers considered it community property and routinely hunted and cut firewood. The shallow soil stunted the tree growth, although hardwoods still predominated.

"Father, look at that old tree over there. That windstorm we had a week ago must have toppled it. Look at how the rock shaped those roots. How old do you think that tree is?"

"Not sure, George. It looks solid enough. Maybe we should cut it up for fuel. Let's take a closer look."

The two men approached the mammoth trunk. "This thing must be two and a half or three feet in diameter." George began calculating how they might drag it out.

"George, Look here. There is a skeleton in these branches! It looks like someone tried living in it. Look, his legs are broken. He must have fallen and climbed into the tree for protection from wo."

"Father, doesn't this look like Wolf's old hat?"

"I think it is. Hey, over here is an old box. Oh my, it's full of money."

"What are we going to do?"

"Well, the money isn't ours. We don't want it stolen, so we'll take it. We need to tell our police officer. I'm sure there is a law about these things."

It didn't take Norris long. "Luis, you think this is Wolf?"

"Can't be sure. Wolf has been gone for several years, but that hat looks like his."

Norris scratched his head. "I think he died naturally, falling and then starving. I can't be sure, but it doesn't appear like murder, especially since his money box is intact. He has no family or kin and has been missing without anyone looking for him. You found the money. It's yours."

Most villagers didn't go to Wolf's funeral in Luis' parlor. Luis buried Wolf in the village cemetery, close to Pa. Afterward, Luis and Emma walked home.

"Emma, Wolf was like family. He was a refugee, only from things that only he knew about. In many ways, he was like us."

"Yes, Luis. That is so true. I'm glad we laid him near our other family."

"I hope Wolf finally is at rest. What should we do with Wolf's money?"

"Luis, we can't keep the money. Wolf earned it, and it was his. It's not right for us to keep it."

"You're right, Emma. What should we do with it?"

"Let's give it to the preacher and tell him to use it to help people like Wolf. It seems like drifters are always making their way down the corduroy road. Maybe the preacher can use it to give them a meal?"

"Good idea. Here's the church. We can stop and talk to the preacher."

A few days later, Luis bent over to attach the milking machine when the cow decided it had other plans and kicked him in the head. George found him and carried him inside, but it was too late. There was one more funeral in the parlor, attended by most of the town.

Now they are all gone. I'm the only one left. I don't work very well. The furnace wanted to cry but couldn't.

George was very pensive the day after Luis' funeral. "Anna, with my Father gone, none are left from the old country. Pa did well, and my father did, too. Now it's up to me. Their life under the Barron and their flight toughened them up. They always treated people right. They never forgot their escape and always looked for those needing help. What about us? What will we do with what they gave us?"

Anna smiled and put her hand on George's shoulder. "You'll do fine maintaining the family traditions."

The listening furnace agreed with Anna.

Emma slowly turned household duties to Anna and began spending her time playing with her grandchildren. Her arthritis hurt terribly, and she had trouble walking but never complained. The furnace knew of her pain because she always warmed her hands near a radiator. It did the best it could to keep the house comfortable for her.

Furnace duties fell on George. George noticed that his February load of coal looked different. *We won't need as much of this coal as usual. I wonder why it burns so hot? And all that ash!*

The furnace didn't like the new coal, longing for the old coal. *This batch hurts when George feeds me.*

About a week later, George couldn't see several grates through the firebox door. *Oh-oh, it looks like a couple of grates burned through.* He shook the grates, only to see another crumble and fall into the ash bin.

"Not good. I'm out of grates." He told the furnace, who desperately wanted to say "I'm sorry" but, of course, could not.

George went down to the supply store. "Morning, Cas."

"Morning, George. What brings you here this early?"

"I had several grates burn completely through."

"Hmm, well, let me see if I can order some. Hmm. Bad news. The catalog doesn't show replacements."

"What should I do?"

"Let me telegraph the manufacturer to see if we can get some. Meanwhile, I can only suggest you do the best you can."

Two days later, Cas knocked on George's door.

"Hello, Cas, come on in."

"Thanks, George. I can't stay long; I need to return to the store. My boy's a good man, but I don't feel comfortable being gone. You understand how it is."

"Sure do. Your store is like my farm, a family member, just like your kids. We need to take care of it."

"Well, I heard from the foundry about those grates. They don't make them anymore because the casting mold broke. The company decided to discontinue making them due to a lack of demand. They don't have any left in their warehouse. I also talked to the blacksmith about possibly making replacements. He didn't think he had the skills since they have rather complicated shapes."

"Okay." George stretched the word out, thinking about what to do next.

"I checked, and you can get a new furnace in less than a week. The only thing is that it won't be the wood and coal type but a propane one. Did you see that new place by the railroad siding? Those tanks are for propane. The owner drives around and fills home tanks, and you set the thermostat to the desired temperature. It's a dial-like thing you adjust. If you want it warmer, you dial it in. If you don't want it as hot, again, you only dial it in. Never any ash to carry out or wood to cut. It responds quickly, not like the coal burners.

"The catch is cost. Propane is more expensive than coal, and you already have the wood. Most customers adjust the temperature based on what they're doing. When everyone is in the fields, they set the temperature cooler. It immediately makes less heat and saves on fuel."

"I don't see much choice here."

"It's worse. The railroad just told me they're stopping coal deliveries after this winter. That last batch was pitiful as it had a lot of dirt, and no one was satisfied. Someone called it hard coal for melting iron ore to make steel or something like that."

"Looks like you should order a new furnace."

"Will do that. There'll be a waiting list as soon as word about the coal gets out. You have an emergency, and we need to install one immediately."

"Yes, you're right. Thanks."

It took three weeks to arrive, and in the meantime, another grate failed. Only two were left in the furnace, making George even more careful. It felt sick, but there was nothing it could do. Once Cas received the new furnace, George let the fire die out and cleaned the ashes from the ash bin before Cas arrived to help with the replacement. Cas started by examining the firebox.

"Hey, this thing's wet! Look, the water jacket leaks." Cas shined his light around the box, examining the water chest. "In fact, you have several leaks. It looks like the metal burned through here, here, and here. They look as if they have been here for some time. Did the furnace need more water than usual? These leaks could have been why it didn't heat as well. I am surprised you didn't notice the leaks, but I guess they were small enough that you didn't see them before the fire evaporated the water. Well, we're replacing it anyway."

Now, the furnace felt terrible. *Those leaks must have caused my aches,* it thought.

George got his tools, and the two men dismantled the furnace. The reservoir crumbled when they disconnected it, and their wrenches twisted rusty pipes into shards. The furnace screeched in pain as they undid connections, which the two men thought were only rusty metal scraping against rusty metal. Pa had installed heavy-gauge screwed piping, but the circulating water had severely corroded the piping into paper-thin walls. The red, rusty water made a mess on the floor, and something in the water stunk horribly.

Cas put a wrench on the hot-water header before it branched to the radiators and pulled, shattering the pipe like glass. The shrieking noise echoed through the concrete basement.

"George, these pipes sound like this is the first time anyone has taken these joints apart. Doing this work all day would do something bad to you."

"Well, Cas, how old are they? Pa put them in many years ago, and we never had a reason to take most apart. They held up well, considering how long they've been here. Pa would be proud to know how they lasted.

George looked at his friend, "Let's go upstairs and see if we can disconnect the radiators. If we can't, I have more problems."

Fortunately, the radiators were in good condition. They carefully disconnected the pipes and pushed them through the floor. They installed the new furnace and reservoir and started reconnecting the radiators. Luckily, Cas had enough piping to finish the job.

"George, how about installing a mud filter in the fill line?"

"That sounds like a good idea. You have one?"

"I do. I suspected you might want one, so I brought it with me. Be sure to clean it after every use. Here's how. It doesn't have to be spotless, but fill water must easily get through it."

The next day, George dug a trench in the frozen ground to where the propane tank would sit. It was hard to break the frozen-solid ground with a pick-ax before scooping the chunks with his shovel. Dark fell before he finished. That night, his family huddled around their stove for warmth, and immediately after supper, they all snuggled under piles of comforters in bed.

As George lay in bed, he sensed something was missing from the house, a presence always there, but no one noticed, and everyone took it for granted. He shook his head, thinking, *you're imagining things* and burrowed deeper under his comforter.

They set the propane tank the next day, and the propane man checked the connections before filling the tank. Once satisfied, he started the new furnace to begin heating water. George went from radiator to radiator, bleeding air and steam, refilling the reservoir, and checking the thermostat. Cas recommended putting the thermostat in the parlor since it was central to the house. George adjusted the temperature setting before severely warning the family not to touch it. It didn't take long before every room was comfortable.

The next day, George walked outside to the twisted metal pile where they had tossed the old furnace and junk piping in a disorderly heap. The workers had been more concerned about efficiency than neatness.

"Well, Mr. Furnace, as Pa would say, you did your job well all these years. You saw many changes, first Pa, then my Father, and now me. Three generations fed you wood and coal, all to warm the family. I don't know what we would have done without you. My Father told me how hard it was to keep their old country shack warm with the fireplace.

"I heard Pa tell you all his troubles, but I think you already knew because your radiators are everywhere. Our little family won't be the same without you. We worked together, cutting and splitting wood. Even Wolf helped. I'll miss that. Well done, Mr. Furnace, well done.

"We'll send you to the recycling place, and they'll turn you into something new. Who knows what that might be, perhaps a new tractor, railroad rails, or a new furnace? Wouldn't that be wonderful? I'm glad Pa didn't see this. You were almost a part of him. Why were you so important to him? He was a tough old bear, not given to showing emotion except when angry. But it sounded like he showed you his emotion. He sure liked spending time with you, as did my grandmother. You were a part of the family from the old country, the way they talked.

"Eh, what am I becoming, sentimental over iron? I sound like Pa. He thought you had a soul or something. Well, Mr. Furnace, goodbye and good luck to you."

The exhausted furnace was pleased that his family appreciated what he did; if possible, he would have cried. Knowing the new furnace used his radiators was comforting. But the furnace didn't believe the new unit had the personality it needed. It just wanted to do its job but not be part of the family. *Young'uns,* it thought. *They are too career-oriented and don't understand their family roles.*

Later, George loaded the metal on his wagon and pulled behind the supply store. He and Cas unloaded the scrap onto a pile of old, broken farm equipment and other discarded iron. Cas gave George a little credit for the metal value, and then George was gone. The furnace felt alone, scared, and no longer loved while a soft drizzle wet the scrap. What wasn't rusty now started rusting.

Later that year, Cas loaded the metal onto a beat-up railroad scrap car. The furnace started the scary return to the foundry to begin its new life.

ENDNOTES

[1] NKJV